Nothing Could Be Finer Than a Crisis That Is Minor in the Morning

Nothing Could Be Finer Than a Crisis That Is Minor in the Morning

Charles Osgood

 An Owl Book

Holt, Rinehart and Winston
New York

Copyright © 1979 by CBS, Inc.
All rights reserved, including the right to reproduce
this book or portions thereof in any form.
Published by Holt, Rinehart and Winston,
383 Madison Avenue, New York, New York 10017.
Published simultaneously in Canada by Holt, Rinehart and
Winston of Canada, Limited.

Library of Congress Cataloging in Publication Data
Osgood, Charles.
    Nothing could be finer than a crisis that is minor
in the morning.
    I. Title
AC8.078 081   79-14377
ISBN Hardbound: 0-03-047646-1
ISBN Paperback: 0-03-057646-6

First published in hardcover by Holt, Rinehart and Winston in 1979.
First Owl Book Edition—1980.

Designer: Amy Hill
Printed in the United States of America
10 9 8 7 6 5 4 3 2 1

To Theodor Geisel (Dr. Seuss)
Who gave me a new way to look at the neuss

Contents

Animals

Plants

Important News

Lawsuits

Words and Numbers

Military

War and Peace

Seasons and Holidays

Politics and Bureaucracy

Man and His Monuments

Advice and Self-Help

Preface

When I was a little kid in Baltimore, I used to get up early in the morning to deliver the news to the people on my news-paper route. I used to think then, when I was nine or ten years old, how nice it would be to grow up and have a grown-up job and lie abed until seven or seven-thirty in the morning the way grown-up men do.

Now that I am grown up and slightly over the hill, what I do is get up early in the morning to deliver the news to the people on my CBS Radio route. I still think sometimes how nice it will be to grow up and have a grown-up job.

In the meantime, what I've come to suspect is that there really isn't any job more satisfying than this one. While most Americans are still sleeping, I get to survey the world, to read the overnight wire services, hear the pieces that our overseas correspondents file, sometimes talk with them and with news makers in the course of writing an hourly network radio newscast and selecting a topic for my daily "News-break" broadcast.

It isn't always the big important story of the day I choose. Often the events that are most interesting to me are the ones off the the beaten path. The people involved in those stories are at least as fascinating as the politicians and officials, who tend to hog the headlines.

Most of the pieces in this book were prepared for "News-break." They are therefore real news stories. The people are real people, and the events are real events, unless otherwise indicated. The pieces were meant to be broadcast on the same day they were written, usually in the same hour. Sometimes they were ripped out of the typewriter only seconds before air time. I mention this so that the reader will make the necessary allowances. If there are passages here and there that seem now not to make much sense, perhaps time has rendered them so. Or just possibly they did not make much sense to begin with.

I'm O.K. You're O.K.
O.K. is what we two are.
But as between the two of us
I'm more O.K. than you are.

I'm O.K. You're O.K.
There's nothing that we lack
We're both O.K. O.K. O.K.!
Now please get off my back!

People

Chollie's Follies

Prince Charles is a charming fellow, intelligent and tall,
Though I've never told him hello, nor met the man at all.
And despite the gulf that separates the royal prince and me,
There is one thing that we two have in common, don't you see.
Oh, I'm not invited to his balls, his parties, or his parleys.
The Prince and I are similar in that we both are Charlies.
Ah, the world is full of Charlies; there's a kind of Charlie craze.
Every Tom, Dick, and Harry is a Charlie nowadays.
There's a plethora of Charlies, a surfeit and a glut.
And it's all right that there are so many Charlies with us, but
There are certain usages that tire and fatigue,
And it's time to form an Anti-Charlie Defamation League.

It's fine to have a Charles as a prince.
What makes us Charlies really wince
Are Charlie fish and Charlie beasts
That are not royal in the least.
I'd gladly write a Charlie ode
To Charles Kuralt out on the road.
And Charlie Collingwood to me
Is dignified as he can be.

The name of Charlie does abound,
And Charlies can be duly found
Of every stripe and walk of life;
A Charlie's married to my wife.
Some are the gentlest of men,
Like Charlie Colson, born again.
And some have not behaved so well,
Like Charlie Manson in his cell.
And baseball has seen better days
Since Charles O. Finley of the A's.
The O's for owner, and that was good;
I knew it couldn't stand for Osgood.
But someone tell me why, oh why,
When naming something people try

To make it sound so cute and jolly
By naming something Charles or Charlie?

There's Charlie perfume that they sell
If Charlie's what you like to smell.
If that would make you feel complete,
What other name would smell as sweet?
A Broadway show named *Charley's Aunt*
Was known to make Ray Bolger pant.
And "Charlie's Angels" on TV
Don't seem angelic, not to me.
In fact, an angel's something finer,
It makes a Farrah Fawcett minor.

But be that, be that as it may,
The thing I'd really like to say,
The thing that makes us Charlies mad
And feel as if we'd all been had
Is how a Charlie can be worn
So as to foster someone's scorn.
The Vietcong we did abhor
Were Charlie back there in the war.
VC, thus Charlie, don't you see?
Though victor's what they came to be.
And racially if blacks call whites
Mr. Charlie, that's all right.
Mr. Charles, to be quite fair,
Sounds like someone to coif your hair.
I'm sure you'd give that fellow fits
To call him Charlie of the Ritz.

A good-time Charlie is a fool,
So why not Henry or Abdul?
Why not some other names to choose
When good-time Charlie's got the blues?
He may have had a fall or strain,
A muscle pull or ankle sprain.
But that would never do of course;
It's got to be a Charlie horse.

Sorry, Charlie, you're a fish,
Not good enough to get your wish.
Not sorry, Hector, sorry, Joe,
Not sorry, Robert, no no no.
The tuna not fit for the can
Is always Charlie. Charlie Chan
Would quote Confucius, lots of fun;
Called his own son Number One.
He'd only name him for a tuna
If he had called him Charlie junior.

His Royal Highness, good Prince Charles,
Is not supposed to get in quarrels.
And likely that would be the nub
To keep him from my Charlie Club.
But one day, though, we'll be in luck
For no one calls a king, King Chuck.

The Demon Work

President Jimmy Carter has told his Cabinet people that he does not
want them to work too hard. That's right. There's the temptation,
he said, when you're the head of a big department, to start early
and to work late every day and take work home with you. You
neglect your wife and kids while you hold or attend meetings and
make or take home calls and read or write reports. Well, Mr.
Carter says he doesn't want his people doing that. Oh, there may
be times, he says, when a little extra push may be required to
meet an emergency of some sort, but he does not want the people in his Cabinet to become workaholics. "You will be so
much more useful to me and to the country," he told them, "if
you do have some recreation, get some exercise, see your children
and your spouses."

Pity the workhorse. Do not hate him, please,
For workaholism is a disease . . .
A sickness that ruins so many lives,
That causes such grief between husbands and wives.

It's a tricky disease, for it acts so insidious.
But then, what it does is just awful and hideous.
It starts out as nothing, and then as you slip,
More and more work gets you caught in its grip.

You start off to work every day in the morning,
When suddenly, one day, without any warning,
Some little thing snaps in the back of your brain
And you start reading briefings while still on the train.

Instead of just dozing or reading a book
Its memos and letters at which you now look.
As time passes by, the disease then progresses.
More matters require your noes and your yesses.

There's not enough time for what you must decide,
So an earlier train you begin then to ride.

You set the alarm by the side of your bed,
And visions of meetings then dance in your head.

You don't go to movies, you don't watch TV,
Or listen to radio—not even to me!
You just work and you work, every possible minute.
The day doesn't seem to have time enough in it.

You stay late at the office, 'til six or 'til seven.
And then it gets worse—'til nine, ten, and eleven.
You begin to think all your employees are lazy.
And they shake their heads, thinking it's you who's gone crazy.

Your social life drops down to nothing at all.
Your phone's always busy whenever friends call.
Until after a while your friends no longer bother
Your kids wonder what has become of their father.

And your poor and long-suffering partner, your wife,
Tries to explain what work's done to your life.
But by now everybody will probably find
That work has obsessed you and rotted your mind.

And what many a wife has been driven to do
Is to take up the evil, and start working, too.
You take a vacation, but then, like a jerk,
Somewhere in your suitcase you've hidden some work.

You sneak from the bedroom the very first night
And go into the bathroom and switch on the light.
And there, very quietly, lest you get caught,
You begin to read somebody's monthly report.

Or you go to some island and out on the beach,
You draft your next statement or policy speech.
But we aren't as all-fired big as we think.
Relax in a chair! Settle down! Have a drink!

It's okay to goof off now and then and to frolic.
It's far better than being a sad workaholic.

You must take the pledge, for nobody can force you,
The most they can do is to say they'll divorce you.

But sure as you swear that you'll act like a bum,
An urge to achieve, to accomplish, will come.
But if you can fight it, the feeling then passes.
Work is the curse of the leisurely classes.

Brothers and sisters, enough is enough.
As for me, I won't touch a drop of the stuff.

One of Those Days

Grace under pressure. Courage in the crunch.
That's the tale we tell today of Nashville's Arnold Bunch.

Bunch got up one morning and found to his dismay
He had a little problem with which to start the day.
Some water in the basement had somehow come to seep.
Now he had a lake down there of water one inch deep.

Now, Bunch is not a plumber. He's no expert, so to speak.
But he came to the conclusion that the washer had a leak.
So he took apart the washer, disassembled all its parts.
When he thinks he has the answer, Arnold digs right in and starts.

But he started in the wrong direction this time, after all,
For water kept on flowing from behind the bathroom wall.
The washer wasn't hooked up now, but still the flood kept coming.
So Bunch attacked the bathroom wall to find the faulty plumbing.

He did a job upon the wall. He tore the whole thing out.
But once again, his certainty turned quickly into doubt,
For though the washer and the wall were now reduced to ruin,
The leak he hoped to find and fix, well, that was nothin' doin'.

He turned to the hot water heater, and there he found the worst.
It had become a fountain, for the heater was what burst.
Which meant, of course, that now he knew his shower would be
    cold.
And so, another chapter in the story can be told.

For while he took his shower, turning blue, of course, and
    shivering,
Waiting for the heater parts he thought they'd be delivering,
The lights went out quite suddenly, and now, the truth to tell,
Arnold was not only wet and cold, but lost as well.

He groped his way, the best he could, to the circuit-breaker panel.
There to find another find that turned his mind to flannel.

There was no circuit breaker now, it wasn't there at all—
The doggoned thing had somehow burned and melted off the wall.

This sort of thing gets to a man and tests resources inner,
For Arnold Bunch expected guests that evening for dinner.
And things around the house were not quite what you'd call the
    best,
For making someone feel as if he were a welcome guest.

But Arnold didn't cancel out or tell them not to come,
Which, looking back, he may now think was just a little dumb.
But people do dumb things, you know. All people sometimes will.
So Bunch just thought he'd broil the steaks outside on the grill.

A happy thought, and he was glad it popped into his brain,
Until the heavens opened up, and it began to rain.
Indomitable though his spirit may well always be,
This might have bothered him a bit. It sure would bother me.

But Arnold Bunch is not that sort of lily-livered fella.
He just went in and got out his patio umbrella.
You've got to keep on top of things to make your own good
    breaks.
And Arnold thought that bumbershoot would guard the fire and
    steaks.

But the gods would not accept that for whatever sins he'd sinned,
For when the umbrella was in place, up then came the wind.
Before Bunch could get organized with what he was about,
The wind turned the umbrella altogether inside out.

With water in the basement, with all his water cold,
With not a light inside the house, our hero, brave and bold,
Now heard the pitter-patter and the fizzle on the grill.
The fire now was going out, as rained-on fires will.

So he fought with the umbrella, saying things one should not hear,
And somehow in the process accidentally spilled his beer.
Knocked the bottle over, so the beer within was lost,
And the empty bottle, whereupon, into the rain was tossed.

10

Arnold simply threw it, threw it hard with all his might,
Out into the empty void, the dark and rainy night.
Whereupon, in seconds then, the sound that came to pass
And registered in Arnold's ear was that of breaking glass.

The bottle followed Murphy's Law, whose applications are
That a bottle thrown will always find your next-door neighbor's
    car.
Right on through the windshield, which then of course was
    shattered.
But somehow, to Arnold Bunch, it seemed not to have mattered.

He left his friends and went to bed, and that, I think, was good,
The bed in which that day, I say, old Arnold should have stood.

The Devil and Mr. B.

What follows is a blend of fact and speculation. The events described as happening on the football field happened just that way.

One night about six weeks ago an aging pro-football substitute quarterback and extra-point kicker sat in his study rubbing liniment into his aching limbs when suddenly there was a puff of smoke, a fiendish laugh, and there stood a strange-looking fellow with cloven hooves, a pitchfork, and a proposition.

"Blanda," he said, "how would you like to be the talk of the nation, the biggest football hero of all?"

Said George Blanda, "I am forty-three, six years older than my coach. I only kick extra points and occasional field goals. So stop putting me on and get out of here."

But before he disappeared in his puff of smoke, the visitor laughed another fiendish laugh and said, "Wait 'til you see what happens Sunday."

That Sunday star quarterback Daryl Lamonica sprained his back, and Blanda was sent in and threw two touchdown passes, and converted the extra points, as Oakland beat Pittsburgh, 31 to 14.

One night that week Blanda was alone in his study when again came the puff of smoke and the fiendish laugh, and the fellow with the pitchfork and cloven hooves was saying, "How did you like them apples?"

"Get out of here," said Blanda. "If I thought you strained Lamonica's back, I'd kick *you* through the uprights."

But the fellow just laughed again and said, "Wait 'til this Sunday."

That Sunday, with three seconds left in the game, George Blanda kicked a forty-eight-yard field goal, and Oakland tied the world-champion Kansas City Chiefs, 17 to 17.

Now Blanda was afraid to go into the study anymore. But he did, and sure enough there was the puff of smoke, and his old fiendish friend.

"What do you want? Why are you doing this?" asked Blanda.

"Never mind," said the fiery visitor. "I'll tell you soon enough. For now, just wait 'til this Sunday." And he was gone.

That Sunday Blanda came in for Lamonica again, threw a touchdown pass to Warren Wells, and tied the game with Cleveland, with eighty-nine seconds left to play. The fans went wild. Then, with three seconds in the game, the old man attempted a field goal from his own forty-eight-yard line—a fifty-two-yard attempt. The ball came up off his toe, and, as if it had one pair of wings and eyes each, flew right through the uprights and over the crossbar. Oakland won, 23 to 20.

Now Blanda *knew*. Next time he'd find out what was expected of him. That week, when the puff of smoke came, he found out, all right. But would he do it . . . could he pay that high a price? He said that he would think about it.

"Good," said the visitor. "Meanwhile I'll be with you Sunday."

That Sunday the Raiders were losing to Denver 'til they brought Blanda in. And Blanda threw three long passes—the last for a touchdown. And Oakland won, 24 to 19.

And yes, yesterday, with seven seconds left in the game with San Diego, they called on George Blanda, and he made another field goal, and Oakland won, 20 to 17.

George Blanda seems the same as before, but friends wonder why he's spending so much time alone in his study these fall nights . . . why the fiendish laughter seems to be getting louder. Can there be any doubt? It is in the devil's work, and what the devil wants is not just another soul. He's got plenty of *them*.

What he wants is two tickets to the Super Bowl.

The Last Man

In a place called Walhalla,
In South Caroline,
Is a dusty old bottle,
A bottle of wine.
And Harry Fayowsky,
Though it pains him to think it,
Is the only one left now—
The time's come to drink it.
For the twelve other fellows
Have gone to their God.
The last just this Wednesday—
That was old J. B. Todd.

So Harry's alone
They have all passed away.
And this forty-year-old California Tokay
Is his now to drink,
Because that was the plan.
They left it to him . . .
Because he's the last man.

Harry Fayowsky is seventy-nine
And to him has been left
The club's bottle of wine.
He could open it now
If he wished to today,
For this forty-year-old
California Tokay
Was bought by Sam Pritchford
A long time ago,
Who invited a good friend
That he used to know
To invite still another friend
Into the club.
They all owned the wine.
Ah, but here was the rub:

They'd none of them drink it
'Til time's course had run,
'Til all of the fellows
Had died, except one.

Thirteen men, each one
A World War I vet,
And for years, on the
Thirteenth of each month
They met:
Harry, Sam, and Jim Graham,
Enos Abbott, Sloan Dodd,
Mark Harden, Lee Kelley,
Ralph Pike, J. B. Todd,
George Griffin, Joe Moody,
and Mason Duprey.
All of them gone,
Except Harry, today.

They paid thirteen-cent dues.
And just as they said,
Each stayed in the club
Up until he was dead.
And slowly but surely
As that wine no one drank,
The club became smaller,
Its membership shrank.
Until just this past week
J. B. Todd passed away.
He was eighty-six years old,
At least, so people say.
So the game's over now,
And Harry has won
The prize they established
When the club was begun.
The bottle is old now,
It's covered with dust,
But Harry Fayowsky will drink it,
He must.

He'll open it up,
And he'll drink it real slow,
And he'll think of Jim Graham,
The first one to go.
And of Mason, and Sloan
And of Enos and Lee,
Of Sam, Ralph, and George.
He'll remember, you see,
For he outlived them all,
Our Harry can boast.
So for each one he'll
Lift up his glass in a toast.
To Mark, Joe, and John,
He'll then drink to each vet.
They had each made the same promise—
They would not forget.

And possibly Harry may
Feel a bit sad,
When he thinks of the guys
And the times that they had.
And the wine in the bottle
Will lower and drop.
When he's thought of them all,
Perhaps still he won't stop
For then, at the bottom,
If all works out right,
There may be a little more
Wine left in sight.

As he pours the last drops of it
Into his glass,
Will Harry's own life
Through his memory pass?
How the years have gone by,
How the time quickly slips!
Will he savor the taste of
The wine on his lips?
Will his thoughts turn once more

To the places he's seen
And the people he's known,
Like the club of thirteen?
Will it taste sweet to his
Tongue, then, and fine?
Or will time have diminished
And spoiled the wine?

There's no way Fayowsky
Can tell that, I think,
Until he pops open the cork
For a drink.
So what is he waiting for?
Why does he tarry?
"Let me think for a while,
I'm in no rush," says Harry.

Yes, Virginia, There *Is* a Howard Hughes

Some may feel it unfitting to make fun of the dead. However, at the time of this broadcast, Howard Hughes was *not* dead. Since he had not been seen in a long time, though, his very existence was being questioned by some.

Virginia, your little friends are wrong. They have been affected by the skepticism of a skeptical age. They do not believe except they see. And now they tell you there is no Howard Hughes? How foolish.

True, they have not seen him in a very long time. True, the sheriff's men could find no trace of him in his desert workshop. But Howard Hughes is real, Virginia. Real in a way that ordinary mortals find difficult to understand, perhaps because their minds are so little they find him incomprehensible.

But, Virginia, someday you will understand that $2 billion is very, very real indeed, and although Mr. Hughes himself may be invisible, there is something wonderfully solid about a tool company, something concrete about hotels and oil leases and airlines. And all these things attest to the existence of Howard Hughes.

A long time ago, Virginia, a very wise philosopher said, "I buy, therefore I am." In other words, you and I go into a store and buy a lollipop or a yo-yo, and we wouldn't be able to do that if we didn't exist, would we? Now, if a lollipop or a yo-yo proves that you and I exist, imagine how much more meaningful is the existence of Howard Hughes, who buys whole companies, whole states, practically, with a wave of his checkbook.

True, he does have his troubles. Sometimes his helpers fight among one another and argue as to who gets to do what. This makes Mr. Hughes very sad, and that may be why he has flown away from his desert workshop to a hidden place on Paradise Island. From there, do not fret, he will surely straighten out whatever little misunderstanding there may be among his helpers.

No, I cannot show you a picture of Howard Hughes, for in

recent years his being is too fine, too amorphous, too elusive to be captured on film. But tell me, Virginia, can you take a picture of a merger, a stock split, a bloodless coup? Of course you can't!

Not believe in Howard Hughes? You might as well not believe in Santa Claus. Yes, Virginia, there *is* a Howard Hughes. And he lives, nay he thrives, in the hearts of men.

Marvelous Marvin and the
Mad Machine of Monia

There's nothing more rewarding than *helping people*.

Take what happened to Floyd Marvin yesterday, for example. Marvin, who is forty-six years old and lives in Palmdale, California, saw an opportunity to play good Samaritan to his friend Richard Monia, a salesman.

Driving down Palmdale's Main Street yesterday afternoon, Marvin noticed Monia off to the side of the road apparently having a little trouble with his car. "Having a little trouble with your car?" Marvin asked him. "Ya, darn thing won't start again." "Here," he said to Monia, "I'll just attach one end to my battery . . . like this . . . and the other end to your battery . . . like this . . ." And as the end of the jumper cable touched the terminal on Monia's battery, suddenly Monia's car sprang to life. It lurched forward so suddenly that Marvin was knocked to the ground, still holding the cable in his hand. From his vantage point there on the ground, Marvin watched as Monia's car, seemingly with a mind of its own, took off down Main Street with Monia running after it—as in a scene from a Buster Keaton movie.

Monia ran out of gas after about a block. But his car didn't. It kept going for three blocks until it hit a rut; then it swerved to the right and plowed through a chain-link fence on one side of somebody's property. Kept going 'til it crashed through another chain-link fence on the other side of somebody's property, and then crashed into a power pole, knocking the power pole down. This caused the lines that were supported by the power pole to fall, causing a power blackout in Palmdale. They had no electricity there for the best part of a half hour. However, there was enough juice in the downed wire to set fire to Monia's car.

Monia must be some kind of terrific salesman. While police were assessing the damage and the power company was trying to get the lights back on in Palmdale and the car was blazing, Monia made a fast deal with a bystander to sell the old buggy—as is—for fifty dollars.

As for his friend, Floyd Marvin, the doctors at Palmdale General Hospital say he'll be all right. Nothing worse than cuts and bruises and a few possible broken ribs.

But what a small price to pay for the wonderful feeling that comes from knowing you have done a good deed.

East Coast Version:
The Meandering Machine of Menands

One of Isaac Newton's laws of physics states that an object at rest will tend to stay at rest. And there's another that suggests that when an object falls down, it will fall *down,* unless something external is acting on it. A tornado, maybe.

It is not as easy to violate these laws as it is to violate, say, the marijuana regulations. However, they appear to have been suspended—at least for a while—last night in Menands, New York.

Menands is right outside of Albany. Yesterday some time, a man parked his car on River Hill Road, which, as the name implies, is located near a river on a hill. The man did what some say is a smart thing to do when parking on a hill. He was pointing downhill, so he left the car in reverse gear. That way, if the emergency brake failed, the car wouldn't start to roll down.

Last night though, for reasons still unexplained, that car caught fire, and once the gas started burning, there was quite a little blaze. All that heat must have short-circuited the starter wires, because the starter kicked over several times. And finally the engine caught, and the car started up. I mean really *up.* Since it had been left in reverse, it began moving backward, up the hill. Up to, and through, the intersection of Route 377, across that four-lane highway, as people gaped.

V. A. Oberting, a neighborhood resident, very nearly took the pledge when he saw what appeared to be a ball of flame moving uphill all by itself. Says he, "Dadgumdest thing I ever seen." (Volunteer firemen managed to put the fire out after the car came to rest in an earthen embankment.)

In life the things that really happen are often more unbelievable than the things people make up. Even with eyewitness accounts by Oberting, a local newsman, and two policemen, it seems hard to believe a car went rolling uphill backward and on fire.

Actually, of course, no physical laws were violated. The strange sequence of events obeyed all of Newton's laws, once you understand what all the events were.

Even the local traffic laws of Menands were not violated. The town fathers would have passed a law forbidding the backward, uphill rolling of empty burning cars had it occurred to them to do so. But for some reason they just never thought the situation would come up.

The Adventures of Herman

One evening about a month ago Herman went to Gimbels. Gimbels department store in Philadelphia. Herman is fourteen years old, and why he went to Gimbels that evening is the subject of some interest to the legal authorities. And not everybody believes him when he says he was just shopping. At any rate Herman found himself in the furniture department and fell asleep on a sofa there. It got late, the customers left, the store closed, the employees went home, and there was Herman still asleep on the sofa in the furniture department.

Around midnight he woke up and found himself in the middle of the darkened store, all alone. Sort of an eerie feeling, but Herman got used to it after a while. He says he picked up the phone to try to get someone to let him out, but the phone was dead. Pretty spooky. Making the most of a spooky situation, Herman began to fool around. He tried on clothes—kids' clothes, men's clothes, ladies' clothes. He tried on hats and wigs. Then he came on a burglar alarm and purposely tripped it, he says, figuring that would get somebody in to let him out.

Sooner than he figured, he heard police coming, and what's more they had dogs with them. Herman was frightened, he says, and so he grabbed a handbag from a display, jumped up on the counter, struck a mannequin pose, and froze. Didn't move a muscle as the guards came through, dogs growling on the leash. Remember, now, he was decked out in a lady's dress, a wig, a hat, and had this handbag over his arm.

The police and security guards didn't notice him, although he was right out there plain as the nose on your face. And the dogs must have been confused by the perfume smells (or something), because they didn't notice him either.

Herman figured they'd go away pretty soon. But they didn't. They knew somebody had tripped that burglar alarm, and they meant to find out who. Some mysterious intruder was in there someplace hiding. That they knew. A couple of times Herman's nose itched, but he didn't dare scratch. Or sneeze. Or cough. In fact he hardly breathed for four hours.

It was like something out of a Danny Kaye or Marx brothers movie.

Until finally a woman security guard passed the counter where he was perched, looked up, and said out loud, "My, what a pretty Negro mannequin."

And then she jumped about six feet as the mannequin cracked up, laughed out loud at her, and said in a perfectly clear voice, "Honey, you wouldn't kid me, would you?"

So ended Herman's nocturnal adventures at Gimbels. However, there were further adventures in store in court, where Judge William McLoughlin this week dismissed charges of burglary, larceny, and receiving stolen goods, but found him guilty of attempted larceny.

Herman will be spending the next little while at a youth development center. He has learned at least one lesson already. It's dumb for a dummy to make smart remarks.

The Ballad of the Extra 4:30 Special

This is the story of a sick youngster named David Proctor and of a special train that took him, one snowy night, to Nashville.

"Better get him back to Vandy," the Proctors' doctor said,
For David wasn't feeling well as he lay there in his bed.
The heart defect that plagued him was hurting him again,
Despite the best of medicine, the very best of men,
The surgery he'd undergone three times in the past.
"Let's get him back to Vanderbilt. We've got to do it fast."
That's what Dr. Cantley said, and everybody knew
That getting David down there was the thing they had to do.

But how were they to do it in this awful winter storm?
'Though there inside the Proctor house they all were toasty warm,
Outside the wind was blowing, and the snow was piled high.
A peek outside the window would explain the reason why.
The factories and schools were closed. The roads were blocked,
    you know,
For everywhere you looked there was at least a foot of snow.
And, furthermore, the airport's shut; no planes flew out or in.
So the urgent trip was stymied. There was no way to begin.

"But wait," said Johnny Davis, a Proctor family friend,
"I think I know a way to go. If L&N would lend
An engine and a small caboose, from Henderson we'll go,
And make our way to Nashville through the night and through the
    snow."
Now Johnny knows the L&N, for he's an engineer,
And he got right on the phone and he got the superintendent's
    ear.
And "Yes," he said, "I think we can, I think the railroad would."
And the word went out from Evansville, they'd do it if they could!
So later from the depot, with John at the controls,
The engine started out last night with Nashville as its goal.

And David and his mother in the small caboose they tugged;
The Extra 4:30 South moved slowly as it chugged.

A highrail moving out in front, preceding on the track,
A hundred fifty miles they'd go; there was no turning back.
And other trains were moved to sidings. There they would remain
Until the way was cleared for this, this extra-special train.
The engine with the red caboose, highballing through the night.
It must have been quite strange to see this unexpected sight.
Like the little engine in the tale, the little one that could,
The Extra 4:30 South was moving, doing good.

They passed the snowbound villages, the quiet, frozen towns.
The snow had paralyzed the state; most things were all closed
     down.
And ice was in the treetops, the land was misty white,
And Johnny's little train continued onward through the night.
Past the buried stations and the freight yards on the way,
The red caboose pulled swiftly by the engine proud and gray.
Four hours is what it took, the trip they made last night.
And there around the snowy bend lay Nashville and its lights.

Davis took the little train into the heart of town.
The traffic had to stop awhile while the boy was lifted down.
Third Avenue—the place they stopped—was close as they could
     get
To Vanderbilt. An ambulance was waiting and all set.
And they took young David Proctor to the place he had to go,
Despite the awful weather with the wind and ice and snow.

The doctors there at Vanderbilt know best what can be done.
And David is their patient now, a very special one.
Whatever its defects may be, they'll say for David's part,
"The kid has got a lot of spunk, he's got a lot of heart."

Now when you think of railroads and the legends that they give,
John Henry and of Casey Jones, and memories that live,

Give a thought to David and to Johnny Davis, too,
And the Extra 4:30 South, and how that train came through.
And you whose sleep was troubled as you lay in bed last night
By a lonesome railroad whistle blowing through the snowy white,
If you wondered why it had to be, why that train had to go,
Why, now you've heard the story, friend, and now, therefore, you
    know.

Cherry Pie, Please, and Hold the Cherries

Betty Overland teaches first grade at the Hoyt School in Madison, Wisconsin. And last week she asked the kids to make up some recipes for a Mother's Day cookbook. The results she intended for distribution among a very small circle of parents and friends, but so fascinating are some of the dishes proposed, such gastronomic genius do they display, that already in a few days their fame has spread.

Here are a few examples you might want to spring on your family some time soon. Ready? Okay. Here is Freddy Yankee's specialty, a homemade cherry pie: "You make it by mixing a banana, a carrot, and a little bit of soup. Then, put in three cups of sugar, five cups of milk, and set the oven at five degrees." That's it. Amazingly, there are no cherries in that recipe for homemade cherry pie.

How about Andrew David's steak?: "Take one steak and one cup of gravy and put it in the oven. Bake it at one degree and put one cup of sugar on it so it will be good to eat."

These young *chefs de cuisine* are very liberal in their use of sugar in these recipes, you may notice.

Paul Raushenbush's concoction is chicken: "Put one cupful of salt on the chicken. Then you put it in the oven. Put the oven up to sixty degrees so the chicken does not get greasy." (I hope you're writing all this down.)

Shawn Dugan's cake sounds delicious: "Put three scoops of ice cream in a pan. Then put in four scoops of salt. Then put in five scoops of meat. Put it in the oven. Then take it out of the oven. Then eat it." Mmmmmmmm.

If pizza is your dish, Scott Levine's recipe will intrigue you: "First you go to the store and get it. And then you come home and put it in the oven and leave it in the oven for half an hour. Put the oven at forty degrees. Then, the pizza is ready." Wait a minute, Levine, that's *my* recipe.

And finally, for a real tour de force that will simply delight and astound everyone at the table some night soon, try Campy Craig's spectacular, Giant Peppermint Cake. It's easy. Here's all you do: "Take two spoons of peppermint, five hundred tons of whipping cream, sixty eggs, twenty drops of vanilla, and then mix it all together. Put it in the oven at sixty-thousand degrees Fahrenheit and then wait for six hours."

Let me know how it works out, okay?

"Real" Men and Women

Helene, a young friend of mine, has been assigned a theme in English composition class. She can take her choice: "What is a *real* man?" or, if she wishes, "What is a *real* woman?" Seems the instructor has some strong ideas on these subjects. Helene says she doesn't know which choice to make. "I could go the women's-lib route," she says, "but I don't think he'd like that. I started in on that one once in a class, and it didn't go over too well." So, what is a real man and what is a real woman?

"As opposed to what?" I asked.

"I don't know, as opposed to unreal men and women, I suppose. Got any ideas?"

Yes, it just so happens I do. Let's start with the assumption that reality is that which is, as opposed to that which somebody would like, or something that is imagined or idealized. Let's assume that all human beings who are alive, therefore, are real human beings, who can be divided into two categories: real men and real women. A man who exists is a real man. His reality is in no way lessened by his race, his nationality, political affiliation, financial status, religious persuasion, or personal proclivities. All men are real men. All women are real women.

The first thing you do if you want to destroy somebody is to rob him of his humanity. If you can persuade yourself that someone is a gook and therefore not a real person, you can kill him rather more easily, burn down his home, separate him from his family. If you can persuade yourself that someone is not really a person but a spade, a Wasp, a kike, a wop, a mick, a fag, a dike, and therefore not a real man or woman, you can more easily hate and hurt him.

People who go around making rules, setting standards that other people are supposed to meet in order to qualify as real, are real pains in the neck—and worse, they are real threats to the rest of us. They use their own definitions of real and unreal to filter out unpleasant facts. To them, things like crime, drugs, decay, pollution, slums, et cetera, are not the real America. In the same way, they can look at a man and say he is not a real man because he doesn't give a hang about pro football and would rather chase butterflies than a golf ball; or they can look at a woman and say she is not a real woman because she drives a cab or would rather change the world than change diapers.

To say that someone is not a real man or woman is to say that they are something less than, and therefore not entitled to the same consideration as, real people. Therefore, Helene, contained within the questions "What is a real man?" and "What is a real woman?" are the seeds of discrimination and of murders, big and little. Each of us has his own reality, and nobody has the right to limit or qualify that—not even English composition instructors.

How Donna Got Stuck

In summertime the kids have fun;
They laugh and play; they jump and run;
They slide on slides; they swing on swings;
They do a lot of crazy things.
Think back on all the stuff you did
When you were just a little kid.
That laughter you can almost hear
From some July of yesteryear.
Think back, and you may think of how
You'd love to do those same things now,
To feel the summer you felt then,
To be a little kid again.

The story that we have to tell
May strike a chord, may ring a bell.
It well could have been me or you,
And furthermore, it's all quite true.

Donna Anderson's not old,
Not really, if the truth be told.
To someone who's as old as I
It's difficult to fathom why
A person who is still so green
(Well, Donna's only seventeen)
Should look back on her youth as past,
A summer that went by so fast.

And yet, though she is still a kid,
She looks back on the things she did
With wistful thoughts of how it was
Compared with things that now she does.

She's put away the dolls and toys,
The games of childhood and their joys,
For Donna's a young lady now,
And yet she can't help think of how

Much fun it was to be a tyke,
To play with jacks, to have a bike,
A little kid so very cute
She'd slide right down the laundry chute.

The house where Donna was a kid
Was made for her to hit the skids.
That laundry chute was lots of fun,
And many, many times she'd done
The game of sliding down the chute,
And no one seemed to give a hoot.
With great delight, how fine a ride,
To get into that chute and slide.

But that, of course, was long ago,
At least it seemed to Donna so,
When this past weekend she returned
To see in light of all she's learned
The house in old Seattle town
That had the chute she once slid down.
And memories came flooding back,
Of images there was no lack.
And she decided there and then
She'd feel that feeling once again.

And so, although she should have not,
Into the laundry chute she got,
Prepared to slide and feel the same
As when she used to play that game
In times gone by, in days of yore,
She wanted it just one time more.
But here's the rub; she had bad luck—
And Donna Anderson got stuck,
Stuck between the top and bottom,
Regrets? Why, yes, old Donna's got 'em.
For here she was, no longer young,
Between those floors so badly hung,
Trapped by old nostalgia's snare,
She did not slide but stuck right there.

Some other people tried to nudge,
But Donna simply would not budge.
The firemen came in a truck
To get Miss Anderson unstuck.
It took four men, reports have said,
And Donna's face was crimson red.

They pushed her up, but then she'd stop;
They pulled her up from up on top.
They tugged and pushed; they pushed and tugged;
'Til Donna felt like she'd been mugged.
She felt like such a silly goose,
But Donna Anderson soon got loose.

It isn't so much loss of face
That made her feel so in disgrace.
It's something else upon the earth,
Not loss of face, but gain of girth.
And so, at only seventeen,
An awful fact of life she's seen.

For old time's sake she tried once more
To do what she had done before
To find, alas, that when you grow
On laundry chutes you tend to slow,
And what worked out just fine before,
She simply can't do anymore.

So Donna's loose, and Donna's free,
But not free as she used to be.
By Father Time she has been zapped,
And in her own nostalgia trapped.
Says Donna, knowing what she does,
"I'm not as little as I was."

The Man Who Wasn't There

At the conclusion of the GOP National Convention in 1976 . . .

Last night in Kansas City fair
I saw a man who wasn't there,
A man whom everybody knows.
Where did he go, do you suppose?

There was not even one small mention
Of the man at this convention.
They do not name him; no one does.
It is as if he never was.

Day after day, night after night,
Convention business, talk and fight;
Words spoken hour after hour
As politicians vied for power.

But never did they ever dare
To name the man who wasn't there.
Gerald Ford, who's only human,
Did refer to Harry Truman.

Old Truman would be shocked to see
His status in the GOP
And Robert Dole some points he scored
When he referred to Gerald Ford.

The Ford administration's role
Was spoken of by Robert Dole,
As if the man who wasn't there
Had disappeared into the air.

And had not in fact begun
Whatever Gerald Ford had won.
Great names from the party's past
From the earliest to last!

Alf Landon was referred to, yes,
Though he lost, but nonetheless
He was invited, and he came.
But no, one cannot say the same.

There was no glory they could share
With the man who wasn't there.
Abe Lincoln got a lot of mention
At this Republican convention.

Abe, they quote, speak long and loud of
A Republican they're proud of.
Party praises always shower
On the name of Eisenhower.

But never was it whispered who
Was Eisenhower's number two.
They spoke of Teddy Roosevelt
And how even today they felt

That he was right in many ways.
But never did they speak in praise
Or describe as fine and decent
A president who was more recent.

They point with pride. They take great credit.
But that man's name? They never said it.
It's been a fine convention week.
The music plays. The speakers speak.

The demonstrations on the floor
They cheered, and then they cheered some more.
They spoke of Ford and Reagan wings.
Indeed, they spoke of many things.

But never did they get to where
They spoke of him who was not there.
Goldwater, Rockefeller, too,
The hall in red and white and blue,

Balloons that floated in the air!
Where was the man who was not there?
They could not possibly forget,
No, could not possibly. And yet.

With posters all around the place
Nowhere did one see his face
And was he watching? Did he hear
This figure from another year?

And was he saddened by the attitude?
The words he heard of such ingratitude?—
He'd done some good things, had he not?
To him it seemed he'd done a lot

Beside the things that caused his fall,
But now in the convention hall
No kind words, no credit given
To one who's been from office driven.

As Khrushchev in his final years
Received no accolades or cheers,
So with this person much the same
A great nonperson he became.

Like yesterday's inclement weather
They just ignored him altogether.
A villain or a hero neither,
They didn't mention Spiro, either.

This week in Kansas City fair
They saw a man who was not there.
He is not there again today.
Oh, how they wish he'd go away.

When Kissinger Faltered, His Ego Was Altered

For Secretary Kissinger the pressures must be great
Dealing as he has to with the profound affairs of state.
But there is one consolation—this fact is widely known—
He never need be lonely, for he never is alone.

With him every moment, on the ground or in the air,
Is a senior American official who is always, always there.
The thought may have occurred to you or flashed across your
    brain—
Who is this big official on the secretary's plane?

Who is it that gets to go east, west, north, or south?
And who, while Kissinger keeps mum, runs off at the mouth?
Who is it who tags along, so loyal and devoted,
Who says such interesting stuff and is so often quoted?

Who waxes philosophical on matters great and deep,
Apparently while Kissinger is nearby but asleep?
A veritable shadow who sticks to him like glue,
Who is senior, and American, and a high official, too.

Whenever Henry Kissinger is on a trip somewhere
You'll see in the papers and hear mentioned on the air
A certain high official. Every time it is the same.
They tell you what he said, and yet they never give his name.

It must be very frustrating to go so very far
And say so much, when no one even lets on who you are.
Such selfless anonymity is something very rare,
For most senior officials let you know when they are there.

But this one keeps his profile low, and though he talks a lot,
Credit for his utterances interests him not.
We cannot tell you who he is, but this much we can say,
He used to teach at Harvard, and his name starts with a K.

All the academic honors you can think of, he has got 'em,
And he's said to have an office in a place called Foggy Bottom.
They say he has a portly build and sort of curly hair.
He travels all around the world. You name it, he's been there.

He's won his share of prizes and put out his share of fires,
And critics even say that he has tapped his share of wires.
But this senior official, though his rank is very high,
Declines to be identified—perhaps because he's shy.

Perhaps he is so modest that a blush would cross his face,
Though people who have met him insist that is not the case.
His loyalty to Kissinger has never been in doubt.
They say when Kissinger's not in, this senior fellow's out.

The secretary's policies he's very strongly for
He wants whatever Henry does, and never less or more.
He's sure whatever Kissinger has done is what's best for this
        nation,
For Secretary Kissinger he's filled with admiration.

And he's followed every single step of Kissinger's career,
Through thick and thin, through rough and smooth, through
        many smiles and tears.
That time when Henry threatened to resign and threw a fit,
This senior high official got so mad he almost quit.

He knows the secretary's mind so very, very well
That newsmen have concluded they can almost always tell
What Kissinger is thinking when this official speaks.
It seems far more reliable than most insider's leaks.

No wonder he's allowed to go on Henry's global jaunts,
To be wherever Henry is, to haunt all Henry's haunts.
To express whatever thoughts are in the secretary's noodle
In an accent as American as any apple strudel.

There's no question this extraordinary fellow is a whiz.
So much like Henry Kissinger. I wonder who he is.

The Governor and the Pizza Parlor

The duties of a governor are heavy ones indeed
And an extra little burden that he surely doesn't need
Is to wake up close to midnight to the ringing of a phone
And have somebody order pizza with a little pepperone.

The governor of Iowa—his name is Robert Ray—
Knows much more about pizzas than most governors today.
And what he learned he picked up for the most part on his own,
At home, at night, from people who would call him on the phone.

For reasons that are obvious, the governor insisted
His private phone be just his own: The number is unlisted.
A governor's a busy man—so many things to do—
His duties press him all day long, sometimes all night, too.

For governors must run their states, their services, and taxes,
And they have many people at their doors and on their backses.
Some people hate the governor, and others want to hug him.
And if they had his number, they would call him up and bug him.

And that is why, I'm sure you see, there isn't any doubt,
The number isn't listed, and nobody gives it out.
And that's the way it was: The phone was ringing only decently.
The governor had no complaints—'til one night rather recently.

He was deep at sleep and resting from some governmental wrangle
When suddenly his bedroom telephone began to jangle.
The governor of Iowa, a man with all that power:
And who'd be calling him, you muse, at that ungodly hour?

He lifted up the telephone, this Governor Bob Ray,
And said, "Hello," and listened, and he heard somebody say,
"I'd like to have a pizza pie delivered to me, please,
A large one with tomato sauce and lots of extra cheese."

To serve the people is a cause to which he's firmly bent,
But Ray explained that's not the kind of service that he meant.

He had promised to "deliver" in the days of his campaign,
But the governor had thought that he made it very plain
That what he would "deliver" was of consequence and big.
Delivering a pizza pie? Well, that was infra dig.

But Ray was not alarmed at all or mad for very long.
He merely told the fellow that he'd dialed the number wrong,
Perhaps had slipped a finger and by accident of fate,
Woke up the chief executive of one entire state.

The incident was closed as far as Ray was then concerned,
But it really wasn't closed at all, he subsequently learned.
For quite by chance—as if controlled by flipping of a coin—
A brand-new pizza parlor had just opened in Des Moines
That offered free delivery—no fee or extra charges—
For sending round its regulars or large or extra-larges,
With infinite varieties of dressings for the top:
Mushroom, sausage, pepperoni—still they didn't stop.
They had pizzas that were big and round and pizzas that were
    square,
Pizzas with anchovies and green peppers, too, were there.

And this little pizza parlor, whose name we do not know,
Found that its popularity soon began to grow.
So many people heard about it and began to call
That the pizza parlor's telephone was ringing off the wall.
There and at the governor's: For the governor's people say
That his own unlisted number was a finger slip away.

And it happened then quite often that his bedroom phone would
    ring,
And he'd have somebody order him which pizza pie to bring.
Now, the governor likes pizza just as much as you or me,
But there has to be some limits to devotion, don't you see?
And although he gave his all, all day and worked with all his
    might,
He would not deliver pizzas in the middle of the night.

With such monumental problems, would somebody tell him why
They had put him just one digit from that fellow's pizza pie?

Now, if you are a governor, relief can be arranged,
And last we heard, his number was in line for being changed.
But it only shows things do not always go the way they're planned.
But for the governor of Iowa, now, "pizza is at hand."

It's clear to me that different places
Are more than merely different spaces.
I've been around, and each locality
Has a distinctive personality.
Some I like, and some I don't
Those I do, perhaps you won't.
Some I still feel slightly numb from,
And those are places good to come from.

Places

The Fifty-first State

Without getting into the pros and cons of whether New York City should split off from New York State and become the fifty-first state, let us assume for a moment that all the constitutional obstacles have been overcome and all the steps taken and that New York City *is* a state.

There are several immediate questions: What will the name be? What will the state motto be? The state song? What will the state flag look like? What will we call this place, this fifty-first state formed from the eight million people in the five boroughs of New York?

In a recent mayoral election, when Norman Mailer and Jimmy Breslin were running for city office on a secessionist platform, they suggested calling the new state New York. The rest of what is now New York would then be known as Buffalo.

There are various nominees for state bird. But of these, the most logical would seem to be the pigeon (and possibly, in summer, the fly).

For state tree the lamppost is the only entry.

Although flowers do not exactly abound on the sidewalks of New York, you have to have a state flower. And there are, after all, a lot of privately supported flowerpots. *Cannabis sativa* seems a likely choice. However, it would be sort of embarrassing to have a state flower that is illegal.

For mascot or state animal, some have proposed the rat. However, the dog, for reasons apparent to anybody who doesn't look where he's walking, is an equally appropriate choice.

State song? How about "Smoke Gets in Your Eyes" by Kern, "Help!" by the Beatles, or, as one mugger suggested, "I'm Walking Behind You."

State nickname? The Welfare State. Or maybe The State of Confusion. State seal? Picket lines rampant on a field of litter. Or maybe crossed tow trucks *d'argent* on a field of potholes *noir*.

State flag? Black and blue, maybe. Or crossed purposes in red ink. State capital? Canarsie . . . Flatbush . . .

State motto, when New York becomes a state, could be "It's a nice place to visit, but . . ." However, in keeping with tradition, let us stick to Latin: *"Semper Taxus," "Illegitimus con Corborundum"?* The one I like is *"Sick Transit."* Never mind *"Gloria Mundi."* It's no more glorious here Monday than any other day of the week.

No question about it, before New York City does become the fifty-first state, there are an awful lot of things to think about.

From One Old Buzzard to Another

Every year on the fifteenth of March, just as surely as the night follows the day, just as dependably as the swallows annually come back to Capistrano, the buzzards return to Hinckley, Ohio.

Hinckley is a town not too far from Cleveland, and were it not for the buzzards, most people would never have heard of Hinckley, Ohio.

Why the buzzards like it there I'm sure I don't know. But they do like it. That is observably true. For each year on this day, the Ides of March, the advance guard of a huge flock of these large, gaunt birds arrives in Hinckley. Your standard turkey buzzard is not the most romantic creature in the world. He has a dingy brown body, a dull red neck, and a featherless head. He has an awkward walk and stumbles along as if drunk for a few hops before taking off. But airborne he is as graceful, they say, as any bird you'd ever want to see. His habits are not very endearing, though. The buzzard subsists on carrion that any other animal will turn his nose up at. The buzzard is one of nature's scavengers—useful in the scheme of things, but somewhere this side of beautiful, aesthetically. If the buzzard subsists on carrion, he thrives on refuse. Nothing pleases him more than a garbage dump.

This being the case, one might expect the good people of Hinckley, Ohio, to keep sort of quiet about the way the buzzards flock there. And they did keep it quiet for many years.

But public relations and chamber of commerce men are the same all over the world. Each year since 1957 they've held a buzzard festival in Hinckley, Ohio, on the Sunday following the fifteenth of March, to welcome the birds back. People come from all over (all over that part of Ohio anyway) by the thousands. A traditional Buzzard Breakfast of hot cakes, sausage, and coffee is served in the Hinckley High School. Bands play, speeches are made. There's a spring beauty contest for Miss Buzzard Bait. A local schoolteacher composed a song, "The Buzzard Bump," and a visiting poet from Cleveland wrote an ode, "The Buzzards of Hinckley."

Not to be outbuzzarded, rhyme-wise, here's mine:

Hail to thee, blithe buzzard,
Bird thou never wuzzard.
Go tell Cronkite, Reasoner, Brinkley
There's big news today in Hinckley.
Folks in Hinckley set their clock
By the coming of the flock.
How can you criticize a culture
That annually greets a vulture?

Britannia Waives the Rules

One day in Portsmouth, England, a Lieutenant Slade of the
Royal Navy distinguished himself by recovering the leather
handbag of the queen mother, who had dropped it from a
dock into the waters of the harbor.

Should the Empire and its Commonwealth
Last for a thousand years,
Men will drink to the good queen's health
With their grog and cheers.

Drink to the long-lost glory days
And a time that won't come back,
When the sun you could bet would never set
On that good old Union Jack.

And they'll drink to the British heroes
At Trafalgar and Waterloo,
Back to the year zero
And the gallant men who do

Whatever it is, the moment asks
Be it great or be it small,
In the light of glory, such men bask.
As the song says—Bless them all.

Bless 'em all now and forever
What they've done, time cannot alter,
Nelson, Balfour, Wellington,
And Raleigh, of course, Sir Walter.

What a marvelous thing it must have been
When, according to what's been wrote,
He bought the regard of a British queen
For the price of a muddied coat.

Just a gesture, of course, and nothing more,
And it passed in nothing flat,

And yet when we think of Raleigh,
Why, everyone thinks of that.

Be it true or the merest fable
That the British romance a lot,
It's like stories of Arthur's table
And the tales of Sir Lancelot.

Now what happened this week in Portsmouth
Is another example of
The sort of polite deportment
That Englishmen seem to love.

There stepped from the ship *Britannia,*
The royal family yacht,
Someone from the royal family,
Though the queen herself it was not.

Elizabeth was her name, what's more,
Yes, friends, it was none other
Than that elegant woman of seventy-four,
Her Highness, the good queen mother.

Saluting smartly from the dock
Was one Lieutenant Hugh Slade,
And there passed across the crowd a shock
At a slip the queen mother made.

As she raised her hand in a graceful move
Often made by her famous daughter,
She made this slip and lost her grip,
And her bag fell in the water.

A leather handbag, they say it was,
A tasteful one in beige,
Quite suitable for the queen mother's style,
Her station, and her age.

The bag departed from her hand;
It fell and it did not stop,
But went over the side of the Portsmouth dock
And into the water—plop!

Lieutenant Slade did not miss a beat,
Did not hesitate or frown,
But threw off his cap, got off his feet,
And lay on the dock facedown.

Reaching into the murky drink
He plunged his saluting arm,
Moving fast so the handbag would not sink
Or come to some other harm.

And he pulled it out without fear or doubt
With speed you would not believe.
Without any lag he retrieved the bag,
Dripping water from his sleeve.

And remaining mute with a sharp salute,
Though his sleeve did slightly sag,
Lieutenant Slade a bow he made
And handed her back her bag.

The queen mother, like any other,
Was happy her bag to clutch.
And the comment she made to Lieutenant Slade
Was "Thank you so very much."

"It was nothing," Slade later told newsmen
As he faced the demanding press,
"One is glad to do that sort of thing
For a lady in distress."

It was only a passing instance
As was Raleigh's years before,

But such matters are quite insistent
And impossible to ignore.

And so the story will oft be told
Of a young Lieutenant Slade.
Though his arm be wet, we will not forget—
Of such things are legends made.

When You're Hot

Once upon a time in a place called Ohio, there was a tract of land nobody was making very much use of. It was in Chester Hills, about thirty miles from the city they call Columbus, which is famous for being said good-bye to.

This tract of land was purchased about ten years ago for $10,000 with the idea of using it as a youth camp for Islamic children. There are Catholic and Protestant and Jewish camps, many of them. But the Islamic Federation thought it was about time that poor Islamic kids had a place to go.

As you may have heard, there is at this time in history quite a bit of Arab oil money in the world. This is because there is quite a bit of Arab oil. But this was ten years ago, when oil prices weren't anything like what they are now. And $10,000 of Saudi Arabian money was all the federation could come up with for this worthy cause. Plus whatever it would cost to have plans developed and construction of facilities begun.

A modest plan, but well thought out, and they would have gone ahead and built the facilities and opened the Islamic youth camp were it not for one thing. It turns out that underneath the 138-acre tract near Chester Hills, Ohio, there is an underground lake of oil.

Oil was about the last thing an Arab would expect to find in Ohio, since the geography seems nothing at all like that of Saudi Arabia. There isn't a desert for miles, and Columbus is a far cry from Riyadh. And yet, there it was: oil.

Which does not sound like very much of a problem, except for one thing. The oil is hard to get to because there is a thick layer of a black rocklike substance between the oil and the surface. That substance is coal. A substantial seam of coal runs through the youth-camp property there in Chester Hills, Ohio. This gives the Islamic Federation something of a choice as to whether to go for the youth camp or for the coal or for the oil. But it is more complicated than that because, in addition to all that oil and all that coal, there is something else. The experts say that they believe that there is also a sizable store of natural gas under there. There have been negotiations about this natural gas, and although nothing has been officially made public, one published report has it that the federation has been offered $2 million for the natural-gas rights alone. This, bear in mind, is just a fringe benefit for land that was bought for only $10,000.

Arnold Shahene, the man who has been representing the Islamic Federation, says that some of the offers that he has been hearing are most interesting.

What a problem! Life is just one darned thing after another. First you try to have a youth camp, and then the oil thing comes up. And then the coal seam gets in the way of the oil. And the natural-gas business just comes along and complicates things even more.

Shahene is hoping that the natural-gas people will be able to drill one, two, or three holes in the ground. Well, well, well. And then most of the land above ground would be undisturbed, and they could go ahead with their youth camp. If not, maybe they can take the money from the natural gas, the oil, and the coal and buy themselves another youth camp someplace else. Fort Dix is for sale, I understand, or will be if the Pentagon does the reorganizing it wants to. But if things keep going the way they are, the Arabs will be able to buy Fort Knox, as is, and live happily ever after.

There'll Always Be an Ulawa Everywhere You Go

"Where do you get this stuff?" people ask.

It's right there on the news wires—every day. I swear it is. This one, for example, is a Reuters dispatch datelined Honiara, Solomon Islands:

"Villagers on the island of Ulawa in the eastern Solomon Islands claim to be frightening trees to death by screaming at them. They say they recently killed off two trees that were too big to chop down." (I'm still quoting Reuters here.) "To kill a tree, a village elder creeps up on it very early in the morning and suddenly utters a piercing yell close to its trunk. This goes on for a month until the tree dies, according to local belief, from the shock of being awakened from sleep so early, so violently, and so often." End of dispatch.

Now, this may seem a rather eccentric little local practice, but in fact the good people of Ulawa are only acting out one of mankind's most cherished notions. To wit, that if something is in our way, we can remove it, resolve the problem, if only we scream at it enough.

The Reuters story says this business of screaming at trees is an ancient practice in Ulawa and that the villagers insist it works. Nothing that scientists or other outsiders can tell them will convince an Ulawan that he is wasting his time and tonsils early in the morning.

He, on the other hand, might be very amused to know the things *you* scream at. Although it should be perfectly obvious by now that screaming at the following things does absolutely no good, otherwise sophisticated people continue screaming at them anyway: telephones, automobiles, wives, husbands, children, bridge partners, umpires, broken television sets, employees, motorists, the Internal Revenue Service, Gordon Barnes, pedestrians—anything and anybody that is in our way or not doing what we want them to be doing.

The fact that screaming does not work apparently discourages us not at all. The more frustrated we get, in fact, the more screaming we tend to do. When in trouble, when in doubt, run in circles, scream and shout.

Come to think of it, the Ulawans must be right. New Yorkers scream all the time. And how many trees do you see in New York?

One robin does not a springtime make
One swallow no summer at all.
But a point one can make
Without fear of mistake:
One lark has brought many a fall.

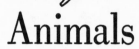

Animals

A Low-key Cat

In the Ford Administration, there resided with the first family a Siamese cat named Shan, described by the press office as "a low-key cat."

A low-key cat in the White House sat,
A Siamese named Shan,
And from where she sat in this habitat
She could see how the country ran.
Now, it's hard to see how she stays low-key
Observing the things she can,
But we'll all be sad if this cat goes mad,
For the fit will hit the Shan.

You Animals Gotta Stop Behaving Like Animals

Animals refuse to read, regardless of our wishes.
In fact, they do not go to school—except for schools of fishes.
So it seems a bit ridiculous to go and pass a law
And publish it in some form that no creature ever saw
That spells out some activity you want them to eschew
Or some definite procedure that you wish them to go through.

A newspaper is handy for a puppy, you may find,
But do not think he will read it. That's not what I had in mind.
If he makes an indiscretion, and no other course will stop him,
One can sometimes roll the paper up and very gently bop him,
Or lay the paper on the floor in such a thorough way
That whatever may occur, why, let the chips fall where they may.

A dog will be a dog, you see. A cat will be a cat.
Animals are animals—that's all there is to that.

You will never see a pussycat, a goldfish, or a pup
Checking out the baseball scores or on the Stanley Cup
Or politics or business trends or wars or other crimes
Or working out the crossword puzzle in the Sunday *Times*.

They are hopelessly indifferent to the workings of the law,
Which is why I doubt that any of them likely ever saw
The news accounts of what they did in Oregon this week,
In Stanfield, where the city council reached some kind of peak
Of legislative silliness in what they had decreed,
In this ordinance, which (as I say) no animal will read.

The legislation stipulates that animals refrain
From sexual activity—allow me to explain.
"From sexual activity—where any human being
Might be in the vicinity and capable of seeing."

Sex must not raise its ugly head or even show its face
On any public thoroughfare, in any public place.

The council, in its wisdom, says if sex must be, so be it.
But from now on, it's against the law if anyone can see it.

Animals may mate, of course, it's perfectly all right,
As long as what they do, they do completely out of sight.
And the council says for violations owners will be fined,
So they'd better just make sure their pets are told and that
    they mind.

And if the owner's efforts in the matter chance to fail,
The council says the owner may well find himself in jail.
The law is new, of course, and as of now has not been tested.
But anyone who wants to try might get himself arrested.

It's high time someone cracked down on how animals consort.
It's overdue as subject matter for some legal tort:
"Whereas these creatures carried on with no apparent shame,
And whereas someone human must needs bear the legal blame,
And whereas all these animals are doing what they do
Without a shred of decency in front of me and you,
Why, let it be the law, we Stanfield City Council say,
That modesty shall henceforth be the order of the day.
If animals must procreate, all that is very well,
But let them be discreet. Have them check into a motel."

The Gnus of the Day

The Topeka, Kansas zoo has a brand-new baby gnu,
The zoo director happily reports.
Bulletin's the baby's name, which is something of a game,
Since the parents' names are Weather, yes, and Sports.

Though we realize full well
That the g with which you spell
Gnu is not supposed to be pronounced
We'll pronounce the silent g—do it purposely, you see,
As the birth of a new gnu we here announce.

For when one announces gnus while delivering the news,
It can be a bit confusing now and then,
For a gnu is but a gnu, even when the gnu is new,
While news is who and what, where, why, and when.

In Topeka, at the zoo, they had not one gnu but two,
And Sports was one, and Weather was the other.
And the gnus is good, not bad, that Sports is now a dad.
And Weather's happy now that she's a mother.

The director of the park is a man named Gary Clark.
He's the one you'll find there passing out cigars.
For a little baby gnu is quite welcome at the zoo
And is likely to become one of its stars.

It was Friday of last week that the birth of which we speak
Occurred there at Topeka's city zoo.
That the gnu that's known as Sports has a new gnu to report,
That there were three gnus now instead of just the two.

Little Bulletin is short—you'd expect a short report—
And his little tail is white as driven snow.
Gnus are antelopes, of course, rather smaller than a horse,
All of which I'm sure you folks already know.

Sports and Weather from Fort Worth—that's the city of their
    birth—
Aren't rare gnus, unusual to speak of,
Common gnus, to speak the truth, so while still within their youth,
They were shipped from Fort Worth over to Topeka.

There were no gnus over there, so they bought the Fort Worth
    pair,
And they studied 'til they really understood gnus.
They were glad to make the space, for it's surely not the case—
No, it's not the case—that no gnus is good news.

Now, Topeka's baby gnu does what all new gnus must do:
It stays very close to Weather every second.
And the papa gnu, named Sports,
Is quite proud, by all reports,
Though I do not know how gnu pride can be reckoned.

So Bulletin, the gnu, welcome there! How do you do?
And may I pass along some good advice?
You'll find this to be true, be you any kind of gnu,
It pays to be polite and to be gnice.

Very often, we may say, on a Monday holiday,
There is very little news out on the street.
But to pay the proper dues at delivering the gnus,
A female gnu can simply not be beat.

The White House Mouse

In the mansion presidential,
There are quarters residential
And stately rooms and offices as well.
It's about a crucial hour
In those corridors of power
The story that today I wish to tell.

Meet a secretary now,
By the name of Susan Clough,
As a secretary very high she rates.
If you do not know her boss,
You are really at a loss,
He's the president of these United States.

Susan Clough's a Southern belle,
An efficient one as well,
And she works there in the presidential house,
And last year she had a fright,
When she chanced to sight
In the president's own offices—a mouse.

And inside the very walls
Of those venerable halls,
Came a scratchy skitter as of tiny toes,
And at times Miss Clough suspected
A dead mouse could be detected
If not by eye or ear, then by nose.

With such sights and sounds and smell,
Miss Clough thought she'd better tell
The president about the little chaps.
He took it with aplomb,
And with presidential calm,
He suggested that somebody set some traps.

But a man from GSA
Told about this that same day

Said the mousetrap was an unaccepted tool.
They had tried that once before,
But would not now anymore,
Since when word got out,
Some people thought it cruel.

So Miss Clough then did suggest
That perhaps it would be best
To set some traps,
At least they ought to try it,
And if getting out the word
Brought reaction so absurd,
Then not to let it out
But keep it quiet.

So some traps were duly set
With no great result as yet,
When much to Mr. Carter's great surprise,
In his office there one day,
He observed a mouse at play,
Not inhibited by presidential eyes.

So he buzzed for Susan Clough
And he asked her to tell how
The war against the White House mouse was going.
What she said to him next
Made the president quite vexed.
She said, really, that there was no way of knowing.

GSA, or General Services,
The thing that made them nervous is
Interior's the one to tell, they'd say.
The Department of Interior,
In no way they're inferior,
Referred the matter back to GSA.

"That won't do," said Mr. Carter,
Who's himself a ready starter,
Please to pass along this very good advice.
They were on a risky path

To some presidential wrath,
And to please proceed to move about the mice.

Two days passed, and then
Mr. Carter buzzed again,
And this time there was fire in his eyes.
He had seen another mouse in his office, in his house,
And his great impatience he did not disguise.

"Call a meeting now—this minute!"
And the office soon had in it
Officials of the agencies concerned.
And what no doubt then ensued,
They knew out they had been chewed,
For the president was obviously burned.

With the problems of the nation
Faced by this administration,
With the power and the force beyond belief,
Was it much too much to hope
That they'd somehow, someway, cope
With the mice of the commander who's in chief?

Could we, who walked the moon,
Have lost our grip so soon?
Could we, whose awesome power is so potent,
Whose eminent technology
Requires no apology,
Be brought down by a tiny little rodent?

They knew what they must do,
And a memorandum flew,
And they organized a strategy immense,
Involving GSA and Interior, they say,
And even the Department of Defense.

They used poisons, they used traps,
They made little campaign maps.
An exterminating contractor was hired.
And reports were duly filed

And then body counts compiled
As by now the operation was inspired.

They put traps out by the score,
Yes, a hundred traps or more,
With bait of peanut butter and of cheese.
And a powder colored green
So mice footprints could be seen
And become a tracking station, if you please.

In pursuit of stated goals
They closed off the little holes
Through which it was believed
The mice might crawl.
It was somebody's deduction
That nearby subway construction
Had chased them, though that may not be at all.

In the wings both East and West
It's reported that the pest
Has lived in comfort
Very nearly human,
And the wings both West and East
That go back at the very least
To the days of Ike and even Harry Truman.

But let history record
That there followed Gerald Ford
Into the highest office in the land,
A man who was determined
To be rid of White House vermin,
And who issued the appropriate command.

Now it can be said
That no mouse alive or dead
Has been seen there for the last few months at least,
And they now can concentrate
On the great affairs of state—
Like coal, the dollar, and the Middle East.

The Kitty That Balked at Birmingham

If you've ever moved, you already know
There's a lot to do before you can go.
With organizing, stowing, packing,
Confusion is not often lacking.
Bob and Ida Moore found out
What moving problems are all about.
They had it figured out like foxes
Which stuff was packed in just which boxes.

Wise is the family that knows
The whereabouts of all its clothes,
The silverware and the dinner dishes,
The towels and the food for fishes,
Appliances and tools and pictures,
Bath mats and electric fixtures.
You only do the best you can,
And you get it all on the moving van.

And the Moores dug in and did all of that.
But then—oh, where was the family cat?
Not a single thing had the Moores forgot.
They were set to roll, but the cat was not.
With a lot of work and a little luck
They had everything on the moving truck
To move to another home and city.
But now they were missing one thing—the kitty.

The family cat of the family Moore
Was sitting peacefully in a sewer.
A neighbor kid told Ida Moore
He'd seen a cat go in there before.
So, the Moores peeked in and inside there sat
The missing member—the family cat.

"Come on out, Kitty," the Moores appealed,
"We've got to move from old Mobile.

And Birmingham is a lovely spot,
And I'm sure you'll like it a whole big lot.
So, come on out, Kitty, because you know
We're running late, and it's time to go."
The response to this from the little cat
Was just to sit. And so there he sat.

Bob and Ida pleaded so,
But the cat just sat and refused to go.
A cat is an independent soul,
And there he sat in that sewer hole.
No matter how one pleads and teases,
A cat does exactly what he pleases.
And it pleased this one to simply sit
While the Moores were having a little fit.

There they were, out on the street,
Their preparations all complete.
The neighbors gathered all around
The storm sewer where the cat was found
Watching as all these friendly folks
Would beg and wheedle, would call and coax,
But to no avail, for the cat just sat
In the cozy cool of where it was at.

To delay the move the Moores just hated,
But they had no choice, so they simply waited.
'Til finally Ida said to Bob,
"You know what I think would do the job?
The electric can opener makes a hum,
And if he hears it, the cat will come.
It's worked out that way in the past.
When he'd heard that sound, why, he'd come real fast."

"What a great idea," everybody thought.
So the opener was duly sought.
But that needed opener of can
Was packed somewhere in the moving van
In one of the boxes. But here's the hitch:

Neither Moore could remember which.
So they borrowed one from the folks next door,
Did weary Ida and Robert Moore.

But the sewer was way out at the curb,
So one could not in the least disturb
A stubborn cat, or make him "out get"
Without a close electric outlet.
Another neighbor agreed to loan
An extension cord that he did own.
And they ran the cord from the house, you know,
Out to as far as it would go.

Bob Moore says he felt like some kind of fool.
One doesn't generally as a rule
Run an electric cord fifty feet
Out almost to the very street
And plug in a can opener completely sans
Any container or tins or cans.
And with the sound of it, just the same,
The cat came running, and out he came.

"It did take hours," the neighbors say,
But finally the Moores were on their way.
The moving truck was on the road,
For they found a way that cat to goad.
Off to Birmingham there they sat,
Ida and Bob and, of course, the cat.

Cats of the World, Unite!

Cats are interesting creatures
With many fascinating features.
Which of us has not been smitten
Watching while some little kitten
Frolics with a ball of string,
Or plays around with anything?

It's nice to softly stroke their fur
And feel as well as hear them purr.
If you're more practically inclined,
The quality that comes to mind
About the value of a cat
May be that to a mouse or rat
Your feline boarder is bad news—
However loud or soft its mews.

A cat is hard on rats and mice,
Which is why it's very nice
To have a cat around the house,
Unless you are a rat or mouse.

This week in merry England,
While the pound fell out of bed,
At least one controversy raged
Around some cats instead.

The story you are about to hear
Is accurate and true
We did not make the story up.
No, that we never do.

What happened really happened,
And it had to do with cats.
Some thirty cats whose job it was
To cope with all the rats

On a certain dock in Manchester—
For which the cats got paid.
They got about two dollars' worth
Of cat food every day.

This arrangement worked quite well.
The cats thought it was nice,
And the company was satisfied
The food was worth the price.

The cats and the longshoremen there
Hit it off quite well.
They were all just one happy family
For quite a spell.

But then the dry dock company
Decided to employ
An exterminating company
Those rodents to annoy.

It just did not seem businesslike,
Thought someone at the top,
To deal with all those scruffy cats.
It simply had to stop.

Besides, he said, he wants rats dead—
A more efficient kill.
When he went down there to the dock,
He saw some rats there still.

The management proceeded then,
Convinced it made great sense,
To pull back the cats' allowance,
Cut them off without a pence.

When the workers on the dock were told
About the cat food money,
It did not seem all right to them,
Nor did they think it funny.

Whatever their own problems were
With the weakness of the pound,
They did not like to see their friends the cats
Get pushed around.

They griped among themselves that day,
The Manchester longshoremen.
And finally, a group of them
Went up to see the foreman.

The matter escalated
'Til the union got involved,
And a meeting was then called
To see the pressing problem solved.

The longshore union's big and strong,
As management has found,
And when it comes to grievances
Won't pussyfoot around.

But who'd have thought the union
Would ever go to bat
For anyone who didn't pay it dues—
Much less a cat.

There are no cats in the union.
That wouldn't be allowed.
So, why was this official
Insisting long and loud

That the subject of the cat food
Was the longshoremen's concern,
Like the wages and the hours
That the union members earn?

Now, stevedores are very big,
And cats are very small.
That fact is rather obvious
And evident to all.

A stevedore can be quite tough,
His talk not always lofty,
But underneath that roughness,
Even he can be a softy.

The issue's still outstanding.
There is no agreement yet.
The union wants to get the cats
The best deal it can get.

It denies there's any loafing
Being done by all those cats.
It's just they're having trouble
Keeping up with all the rats.

What this means for the future,
It's impossible to say.
But if unions get involved with cats—
Conditions and their pay—

Who knows where one day all of this
Just possibly may lead?
What other little animals
May think they also need

Their own collective bargaining?
What union will they get—
The hamsters and the goldfish
And the dogs and other pets?

Will the Teamsters try to organize
Or would the UAW?
And does the thought of animals and unions
Sort of trouble you?

For sure as there is someone now
To speak up for the cats,
There'll one day be a union
That will represent the rats.

And will they be admitted
To the AFL-CIO?
That I cannot tell you.
It's something I don't know.

But anyone who'd turn down
Little animals so teeny
Would have to watch himself,
Or he'll be thought of as a "Meany."

If plants can feel, as some folks say,
Be glad you're not a plant today.
An animal can move and roam,
Can choose some other place as home.
But if you are a tree or plant,
No matter how you try, you can't.

Plants

The Saga of the Furbish Lousewort

Kate Furbish was a woman who, a century ago,
Discovered something growing, and she classified it so
That botanists thereafter, in their reference volumes state,
That the plant's a Furbish lousewort. See, they named it after
　Kate.
There were other kinds of louseworts, but the Furbish one was
　rare.
It was very near extinction when they found out it was there.
And as the years went by, it seemed, with ravages of weather,
The poor old Furbish lousewort simply vanished altogether.

But then in 1976, our bicentennial year,
Furbish lousewort fanciers had some good news they could cheer.
For along the Saint John's River, guess what somebody found?
Two hundred fifty Furbish louseworts growing in the ground.
Now, the place where they were growing, by the Saint John's
　River banks,
Is not a place where you or I would want to live, no thanks.

For in that very area, there was a mighty plan,
An engineering project for the benefit of man.
The Dickey-Lincoln Dam it's called, hydroelectric power.
Energy, in other words, the issue of the hour.
Make way, make way for progress now, man's ever-constant urge.
And where those Furbish louseworts were, the dam would just
　submerge.

The plants can't be transplanted; they simply wouldn't grow.
Conditions for the Furbish louseworts have to be just so.
And for reasons far too deep for me to know or to explain,
The only place they can survive is in that part of Maine.
So, obviously it was clear that something had to give,
And giant dams do not make way so that a plant can live.

But hold the phone, for yes, they do. Indeed they must, in fact.
There is a law, the Federal Endangered Species Act,

And any project such as this, though mighty and exalted.
If it wipes out threatened animals or plants, it must be halted.

And since the Furbish lousewort is endangered as can be,
They had to call the dam off, couldn't build it, don't you see.
For to flood that lousewort haven, where the Furbishes were at,
Would be to take away their only extant habitat.

And the only way to save the day, to end this awful stall,
Would be to find some other louseworts, anywhere at all.
And sure enough, as luck would have it, strange though it may
    seem,
They found some other Furbish louseworts growing just
    downstream.
Four tiny little colonies, one with just a single plant.
So now they'll flood that major zone, no one can say they can't.

And construction is proceeding, and the dynamite goes bam.
And most folks don't seem to give a Dickey-Lincoln Dam.
The newfound stands of Furbish louseworts aren't much, but then,
They were thought to be extinct before and well may be again.
Because the Furbish lousewort has a funny-sounding name,
It was right for ridiculing, and that's a sort of shame.
For there is a disappearing world, and man has played his role
In taking little parts away from what was once the whole.
We can get along without them; we may not feel their lack.
But extinction means that something's gone and never coming
    back.
So here's to you, little lousewort, and here's to your rebirth,
And may you somehow multiply, refurbishing the earth.

Michael Stokes and the Maple Tree

The maple tree was old, but it was big and beautiful and alive. And because it was where it was, they knocked it down.

The men with the saws came and cut it down, and the men with the bulldozer came and pulled out the stump. They were clearing that land to make way for another shopping center in Levittown, Long Island. But as that old stump came wrenching up from the earth, one of the workmen noticed a green bottle that came up with it.

A green bottle in the roots of a maple tree. So the workman picked the bottle up, and through the brown coating of earth, through the green glass, he could see there was something inside. It turned out to be two pieces of yellow tablet paper. On one was something written in Latin, and on the other, a list of names. A list of names . . . and an inscription in Latin . . . on paper in a green bottle found in the roots of an old maple tree.

Somebody took the inscription to a Latin expert and had it translated, and somebody else tried to find who those names belonged to. It seemed a curious enough thing, they just wanted to find out what it was all about.

The inscription was easy to translate. I'll get to that. But the names on the list were not in the phone book, and for a while they remained a mystery.

There were local newspaper stories about the tree and the bottle and the papers inside, and finally not long ago there came forward a man by the name of Michael Stokes. He is seventy-four years old, and he is a retired Long Island car dealer. Yes, he said, his was one of the names on that list, and he knew about the others, too. They'd been classmates at the Long Island Trees School. It was the class of 1906. And one day they had planted a sapling maple. At the foot of that young tree they had buried a bottle that contained their names—thirty-one of them—and an inscription on two pieces of yellow tablet paper. So that was the solution to the mystery. That was how the bottle came to be there in 1971 beneath the huge maple that was cut and bulldozed down.

Now the inscription. This is what thirty-one young people had put into the bottle along with their names one day in 1906: "We shall love beauty forever. We shall always strive for the sky, the planets, and the stars." That is what they said.

"We shall love beauty forever." And the years passed, and the tree grew. "We shall always strive for the sky," they said, and sixty-five summers passed, and the earth revolved around the sun sixty-five times, and there came, one day, the men with the saws and the bulldozers . . . to clear the way for a new shopping center. "We shall always strive for the sky, the planets, and the stars." When you put a note in a bottle and you put your name to it, you must expect that one day it will be read. By whom, under what circumstances, there could be no way to know.

Different Smokes for Different Folks

If you smoke cigarettes, you ought to stop.
But tobacco is still a subsidized crop.
The government frowns on the cigarette—
Warns of its deadly dangers. Yet,
It pays (so the farmers won't go broke)
To grow the tobacco you shouldn't smoke.

To pay the fellow who grows the weed
The doctors say we do not need.
And yet the Tobacco Institute,
In a train of thinking most astute,
Expressed this week the point of view
That what the government ought to do,
If it wants to make folks quit, you see,
Is to hand out still more dough-re-mi.

Statistics and numbers are a bore,
So just a couple and then no more.
Sixty million of the taxpayers' dough
Goes to farmers that they might grow tobacco,
And keep the price up high.
Yet 74,000 people die
Of lung cancer each fiscal year.
And many others perish here
From heart disease and other ills.
The doctors say tobacco kills.

So Uncle spends nine hundred G's,
Almost a million, if you please,
To educate and thus dissuade
From smoking what the farmers made,
The citizens of this fair land,
Who possibly don't understand
Why one hand warns and so derides
What the other hand provides.

85

Half the money is used to grow
Tobacco that somewhere else will go,
Exported elsewhere as food for peace.
Some critics think that ought to cease.
They say it's not nice to ship overseas
Our emphysema and heart disease.

Yet now, be that as it may,
Tobacco business, people say,
If we were smart we would all perceive
The logic in what they believe.
To begin with, they, of course, deny
There's any proof that you might die
From smoking cigarettes at all.
It really drives them up a wall.
And against the wall they have their back,
With the warning printed on every pack.

But at the Tobacco Institute
Their spokesman expressed a notion cute,
Which may not have occurred to you,
But which I'll try to do justice to.
If what you want, in effect, he said,
Is to end up with fewer people dead
And you really think that such end you'll get
By discouraging the cigarette,
Then subsidize the tobacco price.
And that will have the effect quite nice
Of keeping the cost of a cigarette pack
Up where people won't have the jack.
The habit? They'll have to overboard it
For the simple reason they can't afford it.

The higher the price, the theory goes,
The fewer the folks you might suppose
Able to pay the increased freight.
And wouldn't that be something great!
So that only the rich could be afforders

Of circulation and lung disorders.
Now the Institute's serious about smoking,
So one imagines they are not joking.
What they suggest may well be true.
Consider, though, what that thought would do.
We've subsidized our country's shipping.
No wonder that our shipping's dipping!
We've subsidized our trains and rails,
And every day a new one fails.
We've paid our oil men for depletion,
'Til now depletion's near completion.

Perhaps the way to pull the rugs
From under those narcotic drugs—
Enforcing laws is much too sloppy—
Is to subsidize the poppy?
Make it worth the farmer's trouble!
Buy the stuff and pay him double!
That which you would like to kill,
Buy it and just pay the bill!
That which government despises,
Notice how it subsidizes.

The Story of a Mistake

Have you ever seen a prairie flower? Most likely not. For one thing, most of you are in the wrong part of the country. And you are probably never going to see one. It is too late for that. Or very nearly so.

William Cullen Bryant, whose statue stands on the Sixth Avenue side of the New York Public Library and whose name is assigned to Bryant Park, lived when the prairies were covered with wildflowers as far as the eye could see. "These are the gardens of the desert," he wrote, "the unshorn fields, boundless and beautiful, for which the speech of England has no name . . . the prairies."

Out in Newton, Iowa, a man named Frank Pellett has spent the last four years trying to bring back some of what Bryant knew. Where have all the flowers gone? Well, the first serious setback came in the 1800s, when the steel plow was introduced.

The land was cut, the fields "shorn," in Bryant's word. But the little flowers fought back and found some places to grow until the year 1950. That is when farmers started using a weedkiller called 2-4-D.

They drenched the countryside with it, and in no time at all the prairie flower became virtually extinct.

Pellett was a greenhouse operator, and he dreamed of replanting some of the flowers and making the land beautiful again. Wouldn't it be something, he thought. And from private donors and two universities he got the seeds and acquired a two-acre reserve along an Iowa highway. And in 1967 he received a special waiver exempting his project from the Iowa Highway Commission weed-spraying crews.

The rich land of Iowa is ideal for prairie flowers. Once they get started, barring the interference of man, nature will keep them going for centuries just as she did before we came along.

But it takes time and patience to get them started. Pellett worked hours each day in his preserve. But the first year, no blooms, nor the next year nor the next. That was all right. Pellett knew that in time it would happen. And finally, this summer, it did.

In an unbelievably extravagant explosion of colors, Frank Pellett's prairie flowers bloomed with vivid reds, oranges, purples, and yellows. People would drive through, come upon it, and simply marvel. It was like nothing they had ever seen before.

They would stop their cars and get out and take pictures. No chemical psychedelic trip could ever surround one's consciousness with color this way.

One day last week a truck came down the highway with letters spelling IOWA HIGHWAY COMMISSION on the side. A new man was at the wheel. He did not know. And from the truck there came a fine spray in both directions. And for perhaps a minute this cloud of mist spread out and fell like a morning fog. It was 2-4-D.

Frank Pellett's prairie flowers are dead now. The colors are all one—the color of death. He says the seeds are ruined, too. And besides, he cannot bring himself to start again. It took so much time and effort. But that is his problem, of course.

It isn't yours or mine. Is it?

You Call That a Tomato?

Marianne Means, in this broadcast, I heard,
Began with the rather encouraging word
That it's summertime now, and at some roadside stands
You can see, you can buy, you can hold in your hands
Those luscious tomatoes, so sweet to the tooth
That we all can remember from days of our youth.

They are big, they are firm, they are juicy and red;
Not, as Ms. Means rather pointedly said,
Like those awful tomatoes you buy in the store.
They don't sell great tomatoes in stores anymore.
What they sell is an object whose shape is the same
And is called a tomato—very same name—

Round like a baseball and roughly as sweet.
A baseball might be rather better to eat.
In a survey that somewhere I recently read,
The surveyed consumers repeatedly said
That it quite disappoints them, it certainly does.
The tomato is somehow far less than it was.

From that survey there rises a palpable sigh,
"What's wrong with tomatoes?" and more than that, "Why?"
As her broadcast proceeded, Ms. Means then explained
How the current—or plastic—tomato's obtained.
It is modern technology that is to blame
For the fact that tomatoes are just not the same.

It's the way they are bred, grown, and processed and shipped
That has caused the tomato's good name to have slipped.
The pseudo-tomato is made to be tough
Because former tomatoes were not tough enough
To resist being bruised or destroyed by some means
As they passed through mechanical sorting machines.

The folks in the industry currently think
You should pick the round object before it is pink.

It does not even blush, for it still is quite green
When it's picked by the picker or picking machine.
Then into a room the round objects all pass
They're treated with some kind of ethylene gas.
To say that they're gassed would sound rather demeaning,
It's officially called artificial degreening.
And that's why they look so insipidly pallid
As they go on their way to your plate and your salad.

They make growing tomatoes seem terribly hard,
Yet you can grow better ones in your backyard.
Not for me to point fingers, to chide or find fault,
But I think of tomatoes just sprinkled with salt,
The kind that they grow in the gardens down South,
That do marvelous, wonderful things in your mouth.
No, it isn't that something is wrong with your tongue,
That tomatoes don't taste good as when you were young.

It's all this improving that science has done
To make them practical, if somewhat less fun.
And if texture and taste the tomato now lacks,
As if made out of wood pulp, some cardboard, and wax,
Why it's only because, all the experts will say,
That today's agribusiness must have it that way.
To which, should you ask me, I have to say, "Beans!"
I know just exactly what Marianne means.

Look, Ma, No Tomato Bugs

Item: Arnold Brown, forty-one, arrested at his Brooklyn, New York, home, charged with growing one hundred marijuana plants in his backyard. Brown claims he thought they were tomato plants.

When a tree grows in Brooklyn, it's considered so groovy,
They write a whole book and a play and a movie.
For though Brooklyn delights are decidedly plural,
It isn't exactly what you would call rural.

Its people know little of crops or crop yield.
They've even poured concrete on old Ebbets Field.
Of planting and hybrids and plows they know not.
Their idea of a field is an old vacant lot.

But the joys agricultural can't be put down.
And I give you the case of one Arnold P. Brown.
Farmer Brown thought that growing things couldn't be hard,
So he planted some seeds in his little backyard.

And he raked and he sprinkled some water about,
And behold, sure enough, little sproutlings did sprout.
A hundred or more, and they grew nice and green.
The most lovely tomato plants he'd ever seen.

At least that's what he said he was trying to grow,
When a neighbor inquired, wanted to know.
Brown watered each day, and the plants they grew high.
They reached four feet and five—reaching out for the sky.

They got plenty of water and plenty of sun,
But they grew no tomatoes, there came not a one.
Not a single tomato, so fine and delicious,
And one of Brown's neighbors became quite suspicious.

He was, you might say, a confirmed unbeliever,
For the plants looked to him like *Cannabis sativa*.

Marijuana, you see, is what he thought it was,
And he picked up the phone and he called up the fuzz.

The police came around, and the crop it was tested,
And old farmer Arnold P. Brown was arrested.
Brown looked quite astonished as he slapped his head,
"So that's why there were no tomatoes!" he said.

"Of threshers and hybrids and plows I know not.
How could I have known that those plants there were pot?"
No farmer was Brown, and one dead giveaway,
He hadn't applied for his subsidy pay.

Powerful are those who choose
The items that make up the news.
And yet in spite of all that power,
It's much like singing in the shower.
For it is clear from card and letter
That you all think you'd do it better.

Important News

Why the News You've Gotten Is Mostly Rotten

It is certainly true that most trucks don't get hijacked.
And most of the airplanes don't crash or get skyjacked.
Most prisoners in prisons have never escaped.
And most folks you know don't get murdered or raped.
Most countries we know of are not now at war.
And pollution is something all people deplore.
Most wind, when it blows, is quite gentle, of course.
It howls very seldom with hurricane force.
Most embassies do not get ransacked or mobbed.
And most of the banks of the world don't get robbed.

So, why, when we tune in to find out the news,
Are the newscasters constantly singing the blues?
They talk about all of the evils of Mammon;
About war and pestilence, earthquakes and famine;
Distress and disorder, dismay and disruption,
All sorts of terrible crime and corruption;
About how high in government Watergate reached,
And how even the president may be impeached.
It is all so depressing and so hard to take,
That you hear people say, "Come on, give us a break!

"Why are you selecting the bad stuff to tell,
When you could be reporting good stuff just as well?
When a famous man dies, you report his demise,
With the cause of his death and the wherefores and whys.
But you never do trumpet it out on your horn,
On the day that the same famous fellow was born.
If you're going to talk about sadness and crime,
I say sweetness and light ought to get equal time.
Enough of the clouds and your mourning and whining!
Let's have a bit of the old silver lining!
We've all really had it with trouble and woe.
And if those things exist, why, we don't want to know."

But imagine if that were acceptable thinking,
And you were in charge of a boat that was sinking.

You'd spare all the passengers unwelcome worry,
And tell them, instead, some nice covering story.
Aboard the *Titanic*, the captain's advice
Would have been, "It's okay, we're just stopping for ice."
And what if that horse-riding man, Paul Revere,
Decided that nobody wanted to hear
That the British were coming on that fateful night.
Well, history would have been different, all right.

It's a natural thing and a human tradition,
To want to believe things are how you are wishin'.
And when someone arrives who informs you they're not,
You may well want to order that messenger shot.
From your doctor you want to hear happy prognoses,
But not if you really expect a thrombosis.
No one likes an alarmist, but things can be dire
If nobody tells you when your house is on fire.

And a newsman would have to be some sort of liar
To say, in the words of the ancient town crier
As he walked through the streets of the town with his bell,
It's seven o'clock, all is well, all is well.
We could say it, of course, for it's easy to do.
But there's only one problem: It wouldn't be true,
For all isn't well, I am sure you'd agree.
And whatever improvement there is going to be
Will have to be done by somebody who heard
Even, home on the range, the discouraging word.

So, that's why you don't hear a lot of good news
About planes that land safely with riders and crews
And weather that's lovely and earth that won't quake
And government leaders being not on the take.
It's not that such things don't happen; they do—
All the time—which is why they are not news or new.
If no news is good news, it follows (to me)
That good news is no news, I say Q.E.D.

How to Deal with a Crisis

The one thing there has been a very great proliferation of
Is crises, which it would appear we have become a nation of.
We've got crises blooming here at home, and crises international.
Crises that make little sense because they are irrational.
Crises that are major that sneak up and enrage you without
    warning.
Nothing could be finer than a crisis that is minor in the morning.

Once upon a time the world was such
That things you'd call a crisis didn't happen very much.
Oh, we had our little difficulties, problems, and concerns,
But they did not seem to threaten us the way a crisis burns.
A crisis is a turning point, a situation when
What happens will determine what will happen to us then.
Crisis-oriented people, if such people could be found,
Had to wait a good long time before a crisis came around.

But now for crisis lovers it's a veritable feast.
There's a crisis about fuel, a crisis in the Middle East.
The environmental crisis (a few crisises ago)
Is forgotten in the madness of the crises we now know.
It seems like only yesterday the crisis over meat
Made everybody wonder if we could afford to eat.
Get used to it, the farmers said, it does no good to weep—
The good old days are gone when you could buy a meal for cheap.
You've got to buy, regardless of how high the silly price is,
Even if it means another monetary crisis.

The monetary crisis, you'll remember we were told,
Was related to the crisis that we all had over gold.
The dollar crisis was, of course, quite critically related,
The fiscal crisis being something currency created.

The Cuban missile crisis put us at the brink of war,
So we all have been through this thing called a crisis once before.
But never quite so many crises piling on each other—

It would have absolutely been a shock to your grandmother.
The pronounced proliferation has been more than evolutional,
Why, every other day we have a crisis constitutional.
We had one back in Agnew's case, and one about the tapes,
There's lots of bitter fruit around—I think it's sour grapes.
There's a crisis now of confidence, I heard somebody say,
And a crisis down on Wall Street about every other day.

And one affects another, as crises tend to do,
Sort of where you have a crisis you will very soon have two.
Which constantly accelerate up to the speed of light,
At which point there's a crisis about everything in sight.
An infinity of crises come out breathing down our back,
But we'll all be out of energy to bother keeping track.
Whatever sign we're under, be it Capricorn or Pisces,
Gemini or Virgo, we are all beset with crises.

Crisis is so common now, we get a little numb.
Yet, deep inside we have a feeling we shall overcome.
"Crisis" sounds so ominous that here's my little plan,
Let's take the word and just impose the very strictest ban.
And years from now they'll wonder how we managed, how we
    did it.
And there will be no crises, for the law will just forbid it.

The All-Time Number One Soporific

The economy is heavy stuff, important to us all,
But when it is discussed, why, then asleep we tend to fall.
When we hear about the price of gold or balances of trade,
Our eyelids droop, our vision blurs, and things begin to fade.

The GNP and discount rate are weighty subjects, which
Will cause most people's teeth to ache, their scalps begin to itch.
There seems to be a lot of economic news this season.
It is called the dismal science, and for very valid reason.

If you find economic news depressing, dull, and bland,
Attend me now, and I shall help you really understand
The fascinating interplay, exciting as can be,
Between the Cost of Living and the monthly GNP.

Such indices speak volumes and can certainly be trusted,
When they are rightly understood and seasonally adjusted.

These days one reads a lot about, and very much is made,
Of the regular unfavorable balances of trade.
We buy and sell, and sell and buy, there isn't any doubt.
But, sad to tell, less money's coming in than going out.

And if it all keeps on this way, the thing that makes me nervous is
We'll soon be out of money but have all the goods and services.

It is for reasons such as this, so hopelessly abysmal,
That economics came to be regarded as so dismal.
There are problems facing us. By us I mean the nation.
There is the very troublesome distraction of inflation.

We know that prices rise and fall, but if I seem to frown,
It's only that they're going just one way. I don't mean down!

It costs a lot to buy a fig, a flower, fish, or fowl,
And to our grief the price of beef can make us want to howl.
It's obvious to anyone who tries to figure why
The folks who sell these things to us pay more for what they buy.

Regardless what the government's opinion or advice is,
The squeeze results in these suppliers jacking up their prices.

And labor asks for wage boosts as they chase the cost of living,
And employers have to get more to give out what they are giving.
And plants cost more to build today, a great deal more, and how!
Tomorrow will be even worse, we'd better build one now.

And out they go to make their plans, expand, and borrow money.
And what that does to industry, well, it isn't even funny.

In every piece of news that comes the stock exchange is rocked,
For nobody is queasier than somebody with stock.
And yet he does not know what's right, does not know how to
    tell
If this is what he ought to buy or run right out and sell.

The government economists say things are good and strong.
And they may very well be right. Although they could be wrong.
But they are men of confidence and cold and steely nerve
And so are the fellows who run the Federal Reserve.

With one eye looking overseas, where lately we are told,
The dollar took it on the chin, the rush was on for gold.

As speculators like those Arab oil potentates
Traded in the currency of the United States
For something else they like a lot, for which they'd gladly settle—
A certain shiny, soft, and heavy yellow precious metal.

And while the simple folks may feel secure within their homes,
Who knows what those clever men in Zurich there, the gnomes,
Will do to further undermine the value of the dollar
So that all that you and I can do is take our licks and holler?

For Monies International, the monetary system,
Has many ways to make some loot, but somehow I have missed
    'em.

If only interest rates could be more interesting sometime.
We cannot bring ourselves to care, not even when they're prime.
But wait a minute! Please don't doze! I have not mentioned yet
My theory about how to service this year's national debt.
I know you'll find it captivating, not the least bit boring.
But I'll save it for some other time. I see that you are snoring.

Quite often something done for you
Turns out to be done *to* you.
And if you do it back to him,
He probably will *sue* you.

Lawsuits

Yuck Versus Slime

The study of law is a worthy pursuit;
The legal profession is very astute;
It attracts the most clever and subtle of minds;
There are so many cases of various kinds;
And a lawyer or two will be making a buck
From the now-pending lawsuit of Slime versus Yuck.

Slime is a product that's made by Mattel.
If you have little kiddies, you may know it well.
It is slimy and gooey and yucky and such,
And therefore is loved by small kids very much.
Playing with something as wretched as Slime,
Little kids have just a wonderful time.
It wiggles and stretches; it's clammy and green;
It's as drippy as anything you've ever seen.

But Slime's not alone on the toy-product shelf—
It does not have the field to enjoy to itself.
It happens that there's a competitive muck,
A similar product, whose trade name is Yuck.
And Slime Worms, which are also produced by Mattel
Are a whole lot like Yuck Worms, which Yuck makes as well.
So, in feeling and texture, in shapes and in forms,
Yuck would appear to conform to Slime's norms.

And the Slime people say that it can't be just luck
That Yuck is like Slime and that Slime is like Yuck.
And since, they say, Slime slithered first into view,
And since Yuck is a Johnny-Come-Lately that's new,
And since Yuck is so slimy, so much like their glop,
They want Yuck to cease and desist and to stop.

So they called in the lawyers to file with the courts
Appropriate papers, opinions, and torts.
So a courtroom is destined to now be the place,
But will *Slime versus Yuck* be a federal case?

Indeed, if the present intentions come through,
A federal judge may decide on whose goo
Must go, if, indeed, either one's on the skids
As a gooey diversion for goo-loving kids.
Or whether, as Yuck's makers strongly insist,
Both Slime and Yuck can, indeed, coexist.

Each, after all, has a number of uses,
Though each only sits there and silently oozes.
How can a child be expected to choose
Which brand to put in his father's new shoes?
Many's the father who already knows
That clammy sensation between his own toes.
And that's only one of the cute little tricks
Slime and Yuck fanciers do just for kicks.
Unspeakable pranks with both kinds of the goo,
Purple or green, I don't care, nor will you.

But back, if I may, to the matter at hand,
The lawsuit that pends in the courts of the land.
On the one hand, there's Slime, on the other there's Yuck,
With issues of law it's not easy to duck.
And though justice is known to move slow as molasses,
Lawyers with briefcases full of *whereas*'s
Are busy researching the precedent cases
With solemn demeanor and serious faces;
Grown men and women as sharp as you please,
People with wonderful legal degrees,
Learned as counselors, wise and sublime,
Concerned with this matter of Yuck versus Slime.

Back in the days when they studied the law,
I'll wager not one of them ever foresaw,
Nor was there a way that it could be foreseen,
That a slithery goo, either purple or green,
Would one day require his legal attention
Because of some corporate feud or dissension.

There is a dispute, that is clear on its face;
We don't question the merits or facts of the case,

But justice is blind, you will surely recall,
With the scale in her hand quite majestic and all,
And she needs not to see in the Slime/Yuck appeal,
For with Slime and Yuck one can judge them by feel.
Slime, we are told, is a runaway smash—
Its maker is making a whole lot of cash,
Which leaves us with this as we leave you today:
Don't let anyone tell you that Slime does not pay!

A Broken Date

Many is the fellow who's been stood up by a date,
A rather disappointing and humiliating fate.
Tom Horsely's an accountant, and he lives near San Jose,
And he made a date with somebody named Alyn Chesselet.
And he drove to San Francisco, where Alyn happens to work,
And came away rejected and feeling like a jerk.
She couldn't see him after all for a reason of some sort,
But Horsely isn't satisfied; he's taking her to court.

The defendant is a waitress at Vesuvio's Café,
And she made a date with somebody who lives near San Jose.
Tom Horsely, an accountant, has a fine accountant's mind,
And a certain thirst for justice, as you will shortly find.
For a suit has now been filed, the legal documents all say,
In small claims court: the case of *Horsely versus Chesselet.*

They had a date for dinner, after which they'd see a show,
But when the evening came, Alyn told Tom she couldn't go.
Imagine, if you will, the consternation that was his,
All dressed up and ready with two tickets to *The Wiz.*
He'd driven in from Campbell, which is next to San Jose,
All the way to San Francisco for this date with Chesselet.
And he wanted to get back at her whatever way he could,
And his mind began to work, as only an accountant's would.

Two hours on the road he drove, the thought began to grate,
At eight-fifty an hour, his accounting business rate.
He drove a hundred miles that night, enough to really rile;
A hundred miles, thought Horsely, at seventeen cents a mile.
And it came to him right then and there exactly what he'd do.
He'd file a claim against Alyn; he'd go to court and sue.
They had an oral contract, Tom Horsely's lawsuit states,
And at the going mileage and accountant's charging rates,
He figures that he's out some dollars, make it thirty-four,
And for filing fees and paper serving, make it four bucks more.

So he's saying to Alyn, his would-be show-and-dinner date,
Pay me what you cost me, come across with thirty-eight.
Miss Chesselet is quite surprised, no *if*s, *and*s, or *but*s.
If Horsely thinks she'll pay him, why, she says, he must be nuts.
He's just doing it to bug me, says Alyn Chesselet,
I can't believe the small claims court would really make me pay.

But Horsely feels it's only fair Alyn should pay the cost,
At least for time and mileage that the ruined evening lost.
If he wins in court, Tom Horsely says, then vindication's his;
He did not charge her, after all, for the tickets to *The Wiz*.
Just out-of-pocket time and mileage, regular expense,
And nothing for his suffering, for that would be immense.
And that would be a legal case of quite another sort,
Outside the jurisdiction of that little small claims court.
Why, he'd have to get a lawyer; it would cost a great amount,
As any cost accountant could quite easily account.

So, she's getting off quite easily, is Horsely's point of view,
For doing what she did that night, or rather, didn't do.
The case is right now pending. It has not been settled yet,
And Horsely doesn't want Alyn to easily forget
The night she broke that date and spoiled those lovely plans of his
And did not wine and dine with him, and did not see *The Wiz*.

Tom Horsely is a single man; he does not have a wife
To share with him the balance sheet, the P&L of life,
Which Alyn Chesselet is not a likely prospect for.
She speaks of Horsely coarsely, will not see him anymore.
But let the record show, for it's a fact of great renown,
If you stand up Thomas Horsely, he won't take it lying down.

The Toast of Malcolm Scroud

Do you like butter on your toast?
Many folks do, if not most.
Unless they are on some kind of diet
That's the way they tend to try it.
Otherwise, I can't think why
They'd order that their toast be dry.

This fact, while commonplace and true,
To most uncommon import grew
In a certain legal case
The courts of Oregon did face.

Now, toast is cheap as it can be,
In certain restaurants it's free.
But without a doubt the piece of toast
That costs someone the very most
Is the piece of toast the courts allowed
Meant $10,000 to Malcolm Scroud.

Consumer advocates are proud
Of a fellow name of Malcolm Scroud.
In Salem, Oregon, one day,
The records of the state court say,
Malcolm Scroud was one of many
Who ate his breakfast out at Denny's.
Denny might well think today
He wishes Scroud had stayed away,
Because of what then came to pass,
From Denny's point of view: Alas!

Malcolm Scroud looked at the menu
And decided he'd continue
A breakfast habit that was his,
Of many folks, in fact, it is,
Of ordering a piece of toast
That, on the menu, it did boast

With melted butter would be served.
Malcolm Scroud became unnerved
When what they gave him with his coffee
Turned his appetite quite offee.

There on the toast with disregard
A pat of butter frozen hard,
Not melted down the toast to soften—
We've had that happen to us often.
But Malcolm Scroud that certain day
Decided that he would not pay
The tab, which came out to two bits,
And that gave Denny's cook the fits.

Do you really mean to say
That you refuse, refuse to pay
The quarter tab for what you got?
And Scroud replied that he would not
On principle cough up the quarter
Because, he said, you really ought
To melt the butter on the toast
The way that people like it most.
The way your menu says you do.
No, I will not give a dime to you.

At that, the other guy, the cook,
Gave Malcolm Scroud a dirty look,
And put the matter to a test—
He made a citizen's arrest.

You ask, had Malcolm Scroud been bested
Now that he had been arrested?
Not at all, for Scroud was shrewd:
He promptly turned around and sued.
He argued it was persecution
And malicious prosecution.
For he said that he did not owe
The restaurant its wanted dough,
For they had not delivered him,

Through some neglect or careless whim,
The toast as it had been described
There in the menu, so inscribed.

The case moved upward through the courts,
With lawyers' terms and briefs and torts.
The circuit court said Scroud was right.
The restaurant went on to fight.
They took it to the top, the cream
Of Oregon's state courts, supreme.
And what did the supreme court say
In its decision yesterday?

It said, no matter how you work it,
The other lower court, the circuit,
Was correct in what it ruled.
And although Scroud may be unschooled
In culinary matters, he was just as right as he could be.
He did not steal that piece of toast.
And so, today, from coast to coast,
The country knows he won that hand—
The court awarded him ten grand.
Ten thousand bucks must be the most
That anyone has made from toast.
Of Malcolm Scroud it can be uttered,
He knows which side his toast is buttered.

Words are like numbers—
They will and they won't.
Sometimes they add up
And sometimes they don't.

Words and Numbers

Holy Mackerel

You never know what's going to offend somebody. From South Africa comes the news that the censors there have turned down a television commercial for a Walt Disney movie because in that commercial there is a mouse who says, "Holy mackerel!" Now, *holy mackerel* may not bother you, but perhaps that is because of a certain lack of sensitivity on your part.

Holy mackerel, the phrase the South African censor found so unacceptable for a TV commercial, would seem at first to be innocent enough. But the very fact that it contans the word *holy* suggests religious origins. And *mackerel* may be a veiled reference to Roman Catholics, who have been called mackerel snappers in times past—a pejorative term if ever I heard one.

All phrases beginning with *holy* are similarly suspect. With all due respect to Mr. Rizzuto, *holy cow* would be offensive, it would seem, to those who believe that the cow is indeed holy. *Holy Hannah* apparently refers to some woman by the name of Hannah, who may or may not have been holy, but whose holiness has often been cited in perhaps too casual a way. Also of questionable origin is *Holy Toledo*. Toledo, Ohio, is not a particularly holy place, as far as I know. Perhaps the original reference was to Toledo in Spain. I've never been to Toledo in Spain, but I do suspect that, if anything, it is holier than Toledo, Ohio.

The word *moley* does not appear in my dictionary, although it, too, has been sanctified. Billy Batson used to say, "Holy moley!"

Perhaps what the censor there in South Africa had in mind is that *holy mackerel* is a substitute phrase for something else one shouldn't say. When we say *gee* or *gosh* or *golly,* we are substituting an innocent phrase for an oath, but the oath is implied. *Gosh darn* is a double substitute. *Dag nabbit, gee whiz,* and *gee whillikers* are all things that are said instead of saying something else.

Horse feathers likewise. Horses don't have feathers. Everybody knows that. *Fudge* as an expletive doesn't refer to candy. *Cheese and crackers* isn't an appetizer. But at a time when anything goes on the stage and in the movies it is kind of sweet to think that somebody somewhere is offended by the idea of a mouse saying *holy mackerel* in a TV spot.

I mean, shoot, what in tarnation is the world coming to when mice come out with rough stuff like that? Next thing you know your kids will be coming home with all sorts of things like *Judas priest, great Caesar's ghost,* and *jumping Jehoshaphat.* Be on the alert for little telltale words like *drat* and *fiddlesticks* slipping into their conversation. Why, even good old Charlie Brown comes out with a reckless "Good grief!" all too often—part of the deterioration of the linguistic restraint that began years ago in the comic strips when Little Orphan Annie lost her cool and said "Leaping lizards!" for the first time.

There does seem to be an unconscionable amount of jumping and leaping going on in the language between the jiminies and Jehoshaphat and lizards and what-all. And I'll be a son of a sea cook if I can figure out why sea cooks should be singled out in any special way. A lot of people are, after all, the sons of sea cooks, and a lot of fathers have moustaches. The potential for giving offense is practically unlimited.

So be careful what you say that's holy, and advise me, if somebody will, what in the heck is a moley? And who the Sam Hill is Sam Hill?

Rubbing Noses with John EL 29-323

You may have thought that the tide was running all one way. That is, in the direction of numbers. What with serial numbers, and draft and registration numbers, ID numbers, Social Security numbers, area codes and zip codes, *ad googolplex* . . .

In the movie *THX 1138*, THX 1138 is somebody's name. It's a vision of the future in which Christian names and surnames are out, and numbers and letters in, for the convenience of the computers, of course.

But if that is the direction the tide is running, there is at least one hopeful trickle of a crosscurrent going the other way. Within the next couple of months Canada's Eskimo population in the Arctic will all have names instead of numbers.

Project Surname, which got underway a few years ago, is now in its closing stages. About twenty-five years ago the Canadian government tried to get some order into the dispensing of mothers' allowances and other federal welfare programs by giving each Eskimo a number.

At the time, the Eskimo population was largely nomadic, and the only official records had been compiled by white men from different countries, with different accents, different spellings—and the result was chaos. Records would show one man, for example, with three different spellings for his surname: Cownak, Kaonak, and Kownak. All of them wrong, incidentally. It's supposed to be Qaunag.

Other Eskimos were simply known by biblical names assigned by missionaries. John, say, or Samuel. When the numbers were assigned, John of Arctic Bay became John EL 29-323. Samuel of Fort Resolute became Samuel E-2 35-678.

For some reason, in recent years the young Eskimos took to resenting this dehumanization in school records and such. And Project Surname was started.

A Canadian government employee has spent most of his time in the last five years visiting Arctic communities with pencil and notebook, trying to untangle old records and substitute names for the numbers. Each family was asked to pick its name. In one community were three married brothers who were going to take their father's name, Nashook, but they decided against it because everybody in the village would then have been named Nashook.

Abe Optik, who's in charge of Project Surname, says he's gotten rid of ten thousand numbers and replaced them with ten thousand names. Less, if you only count Nashook as one name. He's still got two thousand to go and expects to have the job done by June.

After that I think I'll invite him to New York, where I am known to certain department stores, unions, banks, insurance companies, and government agencies by the Arctic Eskimo System.

Feet, Don't Fail Me Now

No question about it, within a few years the United States will have to abandon feet, inches, miles, and pounds and use what almost all of the rest of the world uses—meters and centimeters, kilometers and grams.

In medieval times a foot was the size of the foot, measured from heel to toe, of whatever king happened to be on the throne at the time. The king was not always around, however, when you needed something measured, so an alternate method was devised for defining the foot. A foot was described as thirty-six barleycorns taken from the middle of the ear and laid end to end. Needless to say, it took a long time to measure anything by this method.

An inch took less time to measure. It was only three barleycorns, or the width of the king's thumb. And a yard was the distance between the tip of the king's nose and the tip of his middle finger when the royal arm was extended. You may think I'm making this up, but I have it on no less authority than the National Geographic Society, which sends me all sorts of valuable information.

We Americans inherited the twelve-inch foot from the English colonists, but everybody agrees that our system lacks the logic and simplicity of the metric system, which is based on the meter.

If you find it hard to visualize the meter, think of 39.37 inches. In the metric system, as with decimals, everything is nicely divided or multiplied by tens. A liter is the volume of a cube ten centimeters on each side. A gram is the weight of a cube of water a centimeter on each side. See how logical it all is? A meter has nothing to do with the size of anybody's foot or the location of the tip of their nose. The meter, as originally invented in France in 1790, was the distance between the North Pole and the Equator divided by one million. How they measure *that* I don't have any idea, but they thought they had it measured, anyway.

This notion of the United States going to the metric system is not new by any means. It was first proposed by George Washington, but the idea seemed too revolutionary. Now hardly anybody thinks we won't be going to the metric system one of these years pretty soon.

We've come a long way from the days when an acre was defined as the amount of land a man could plow in a day. Scientists are the main ones pushing for us to go metric. Their compulsion for precision is forcing us to do things their way.

That's the trouble with scientists. Give them 2.54 centimeters and they'll take 1.609 kilometers.

The Quirks of Quarks

There's a story on the front page of *The New York Times* this morning that contains the following sentence: "The mating of a charmed quark with a charmed antiquark would not outwardly display charm because the antiquark would cancel the charm of the quark." This is an absolutely serious story, mind you, the page-one lead, followed by much detail on page four.

The New York Times story about quarks this morning is under Walter Sullivan's byline, and it has to do with physics. It seems a quark is a subunit of matter, out of which all heavier units are formed. You cannot see a quark, even with the most sensitive microscope. However, physicists in this country and in Europe have come around to believing (many of them have, anyway) that quarks do indeed exist and that they explain a lot of what goes on in the tiny little world of subatomic particles.

Well, now, according to the *Times* story, there is a very special kind of quark physicists are monkeying with that displays a very elusive property that they call charm. It is not charm in the sense of charm school or "Isn't so-and-so a charming person?" This is charm in the sense of living a charmed life. Somebody narrowly escapes disaster, and you say about him, "Boy! He sure lives a charmed life."

And the reason the physicists say that about this particular piece of business called a quark is that certain quarks (about four out of a thousand of them) indeed seem to live charmed lives. They survive collisions that would destroy other quarks.

There are other parts to the quark theory. For one thing, for every particle of matter, they say, there must be a particle that is exactly like it, but opposite, a mirror image or antiparticle.

And that is why, today in this *Times* story, there is talk about antiquarks and the mating of charmed quarks and so on. But never mind all that! We will leave it to the physicists. Let us only take the words and play with them.

Once upon a time, a quark
Was out there walking in the park,

Being glad he was alive,
Hoping that he would survive.

He'd read a lot of scary articles
About subatomic particles
And how they seem to come and go.
The physicists said that it was so.

The quarks live with this certain sorrow:
Here today and gone tomorrow!
Existence is so tragicomic
When you are only subatomic.

Anyway, this little quark,
This one day out there in the park,
Was suddenly severely stricken,
He felt his little heartbeat quicken.

For heading toward him was this queen,
The prettiest quark he'd ever seen.
The way she moved, the way she looked,
This poor old quark, his goose was cooked.

He'd had it now; he'd bought the farm.
This little quark had class, had charm.
Yes, that was it—and how alarming
To see a quark so very charming.

A thunderbolt came from above
And our tiny friend, he fell in love.
The evidence is inconclusive,
For charm is something so elusive,

But physicists are very straight,
And they say quarks, indeed, do mate.
So this quark goes up and tips his hat,
And bows a bit, then tells her that

He is a quark alive and active
And that he finds her quite attractive.
And then he asks her for a date,
Only to hear the charmed quark state

She can't 'cause she's already hitched;
By an antiquark she'd been bewitched.
And by the laws they function under
Quarks cannot be split asunder.

"Hold on there, kid!" our quark friend chimes,
"I just read in *The New York Times*
That if a quark like you is charmed
It cannot be destroyed or harmed."

And he shows this charming little particle
Walter Sullivan's front-page article.
"Well, I'll be darned!" she blushed and said,
As with interest she looked and read.

"Read on, my dear, there's even more."
And sure enough, there on page four,
The story was detailed, enlarged.
Our particle became so charged.

That off they went, arm in arm,
Two happy quarks with special charm.
'Tis only theory, I fear,
But what a way to start the year.

The Phantom Orthographer

Alexandria, Virginia, has the rampant *e* disease.
In the spelling on the signs in town are many extra *e*'s.
"Ye olde this and that" you read, abloom like budding poppies.
And in the olde towne, many shops are billed as *shoppes*.
Authentically colonial though they may try to be,
It's not authentic or correct to use that extra *e*.
And it never was and isn't now the way a person talks.
So, it's there in Alexandria, the phantom purist stalks.

Perhaps he's an orthographer—an authority on spelling.
He may be and he may not, for there is no way of telling.
All we know is that at night, he somehow sneaks about,
And where he finds an extra *e*, he simply paints it out.

An orthographer is someone who knows how to spell,
And may find fault with any misspelling, as well.
And the phantom orthographer, nightly he stalks
Alexandria's old town, its byways, its walks,
With a brush in his hand and container of paint,
And where once there were *e*'s, he sees to it there ain't.
When he finds a "Ye olde," ye paint can he schleppe,
And offending shopkeepers must all watch their steppe.

Like Zorro with sword, who would leave behind *z*'s,
The phantom orthographer *x*'s out *e*'s.
He makes shops out of shoppes, makes town out of towne.
The next morning the merchants come in and they frowne.
The signs they had sported, historic and cute,
Had been edited harshly, and messed up to boot.

The phantom orthographer sought by police
Is elusive so far, and his efforts don't cease.
He hit the tennis shoppe and changed its gestalt.
He defaced their two signboards—a big double-fault.
And "Ye Olde Flower Shoppe" he must have felt heatedly,
For he's visited that one not once, but repeatedly.

They clean off his mark to be *shoppe*, and then
He comes back some night and it's just *shop* again.
The old kitchen shoppe has many a pot,
But the *e*'s that it had once, it right now does not.
For one night quite recently theirs was the luck,
And the phantom orthographer silently struck.

"What's his game?" people asked. "What's the phantom's real
    dodge?
Will he strike at Ye Olde Towne New Motor Lodge?"
The old towne woodworker there in his shoppe
Must wonder if he'll be the phantom's next stoppe.
At a local dress shoppe, a showplace for togs,
At the Old Towne School—a fine school for dogs—
At the Old Sandwich Shoppe, they still slice baloney.
They do not feel their sign is in any way phony.

But they all live in fear, understandably shake,
That one of these nights all their *e*'s he may take.
What motivates the phantom is anybody's guess,
But something makes him really hate an *e* that's in excess.
So beware all ye shoppes in the old towne still,
If the cutesies don't get you, then the phantom will.

You may search the whole world over,
But nowhere will you find
More marvelous a wonder
Than the military mind.

Military

The Admiral's Hat

Listen, my children, and you shall hear
Of the search of the week, if not of the year,
Because of the very untoward situation
That occurred at the Naval Security Station.

Someone has nerve there, there's no doubt of that,
For somebody made off with the admiral's hat.
Breathes there a man who would be such a rat
As to reach out and pilfer an admiral's hat?

The hat of Rear Admiral Samuel L. Gravely
Was stolen on Wednesday. He took it quite bravely.
But others reacted, it seems, with hysteria
When the hat disappeared from the base cafeteria
At Washington's Naval Security Station—
NSS, as it's called in its abbreviation.

Who could ever have known? Who'd have had such a hunch,
When Admiral Gravely went in for his lunch,
That the hat, which he left right outside on the rack,
Would have vanished from sight by the time he got back?

Imagine the staff's consternation that day
When they heard the rear admiral solemnly say,
As he walked from the room after that lunchtime visit:
"I left my hat here on the rack. Now where is it?"

For an admiral's hat, with its brass and its braid,
A rather expensive, stiff price must be paid.
You can well understand why an admiral hollers:
Between thirty-two sixty and sixty-six dollars.

But the problem: to find one employee who's shifty
Out of seventeen hundred employees and fifty.
That's how many folks work at the old NSS,
But which one had the hat? It was anyone's guess.

At each gate to the base, at each exit and entry,
There was posted that day a U.S. Marine sentry.
As each worker walked or drove out in his car,
He was searched, though that may seem a trifle bizarre.

Like hounds on the hunt when they're tracking down foxes,
The sentries peered into bags, into boxes.
They opened up lunchpails, examined each purse.
They've had tough assignments, but this one was worse.

Like customs inspectors inspecting for pot,
The Marines hunted something, but pot it was not.
The offense was a matter far graver than that,
For someone had stolen the admiral's hat.

They looked into car trunks, ad nauseam,
And the cars backed up into a real traffic jam.
They left no stone unturned, searched with such a fine comb
That some workers complained they were late to get home.
In security circles, it's thought to be poor
If security stations are that insecure.

But we understand this isn't new, what is more:
Other officers' headgear has vanished before.
A rather distressing and sad situation
For the navy's own Naval Security Station.

Hats are distributed, dress hat, one each.
To be one down is quite a security breach.
And this one's a dead loss; it couldn't be deader.
Maybe the hat ended up in the shredder.

For intelligence matters and classified stuff
Are delicate, hush-hush, and secret enough.
It does not reflect well on precautions they did
To have someone walk off with the admiral's lid.

It suggests to spy-story and spy-movie fans
That one might do as well with some real secret plans.

It's a bit infra dig and embarrassingly so
To have someone abscond with the boss's chapeau.

Gravely won't comment, but what has been told
By his son, Robert Gravely, who's fourteen years old,
Is that "Dad wasn't mad because somebody blew one,
He simply went out and he bought him a new one."
For there's no telling now where the old one is at,
And an admiral must have an Admiral's Hat.

One of Our Soupspoons Is Missing

It's an awful lot of employees the Pentagon has got,
Some of them are military, some of them are not.
By any kind of measurement, it has to be allowed,
Twenty-six thousand employees amount to quite a crowd.
And all those people, notwithstanding all their fearsome power,
Are very much like you and me when comes the noontime hour.
From the generals to the privates and civilians in the bunch,
They grab a little R&R and take a break for lunch.

So there are cafeterias and eating rooms, you see,
To satisfy the hungers of the folks at DOD.
DOD—Department of Defense—are their initials.
Initials do go over big with DOD officials,
But not the letters in the story that we have to tell
The letters are those ugly ones: AWOL.

Hey diddle, diddle, a Pentagon riddle
To get to the bottom of soon,
For someone went away with some five thousand trays
And some twenty-one thousand spoons.
Eighty-four hundred glasses
Are gone without passes
It's something that simply won't do.
And the Pentagon wishes the twelve thousand dishes
Would kindly turn up someplace, too.

The severe implication
To us as a nation,
Considering what the place does,
Is that something's amiss
In a fortress like this,
Or at least that it certainly was.
For they have as a surety,
Lots of security
(That's what the MPs are for.)
And there's no way of getting

Twelve thousand place settings
And walking them out through the door.

So it doesn't ring true
Does it seem so to you?
That it's something pulled off by the Mob?
No, it seems more to me that it surely must be
Your typical straight inside job.

In the head it's a kick
And it makes you just sick,
As if stricken by flu or diphtheria,
When you just stop and think
That somebody would sink
To take stuff from his own cafeteria.
Yet the Pentagon checked,
And they tried to detect
If the tally was wrong, or so on.
In spite of their wishes,
The knives, forks, and dishes,
The trays, spoons, and glasses were gone.

So they sent out a note
That some officer wrote
Asking all DOD employees,
When they stop in for lunch,
Would they be a good bunch
And leave all the utensils there, please?

All the stuff that's been lost
Is a terrible cost.
That's a thing that's abundantly clear.
As the Pentagon feared,
It had all disappeared
In the space of just under a year.

It's a great deal to lose,
And whoever could use
All those thousands of glasses and plates?

For the rest of their lives
Washing spoons, forks, and knives
Would be something the average man hates.

Disapprove if you must,
But somebody I trust
(One of newsmen's "reliable sources")
Says despite the off-ripping,
Nobody's equipping
His own restaurant or armed forces.
It's only a case of a slight loss of face
And a flaw in logistical mission.
It's a kind of a freak
(Just a leak so to speak)
Chalk it up to a case of attrition.

And now that it's found,
It is certainly bound
To be plugged up and stopped without fail.
But it does help you see how those tricky VC
Got that stuff down the Ho Chi Minh Trail.

The Scraper Caper

For want of a nail, whatever that cost,
The legend informs us, the battle was lost.
No nail meant no shoe, and no shoe meant no horse,
And the lack of a horse meant no rider, of course.
Until, in the end, the foe finally beat them,
Et cetera, et cetera, and ad infinitum.

This morning we offer a similar tale
Of a little paint scraper instead of a nail,
And how that paint scraper intended to scrape,
Got a nuclear sub into terrible shape.
The little paint scraper about which we speak
Had the U.S.S. *Swordfish* laid up for a week.

A commonplace paint scraper hardware stores keep
Sells for just about fifty-four cents—very cheap.
A fancy technology item it ain't,
Just a small hand-held scraper for scraping off paint.
On the U.S.S. *Swordfish*, a nuclear sub,
A very advanced technological tub,
Somebody was using a scraper one day,
Presumably scraping some old paint away.
In the navy, a not-at-all-uncommon job,
Scraping paint is a common pursuit for a gob.

A boring assignment, some people may find,
Not expected to perk up or challenge the mind.
No, the mind is not challenged nor up does it perk
When assigned to a job like this paint-scraping work.
And indeed, in this case, the man's mind seemed to slip
While scraping away at this nuclear ship.
For when he was done in that state of the mind,
He forgot the paint scraper and left it behind.
Just a little bit careless—alert he was not—
And the little paint scraper he somehow forgot.

That scraper, official logs chidingly tell,
Then slid or was pushed, but at any rate, fell.
Just a small little tool like so many you've seen,
It fell into the bowels of a great submarine.
Dropped through some opening, this scraper so small,
Lodged between piston and cylinder wall
Of a torpedo launcher, between them it crammed,
And the launcher became quite impossibly jammed.

So, into the water some divers then dove,
To locate and deal with the trouble they strove.
With a submarine torch and a forty-ton jack
They struggled to move it forward or back.
But the scraper was so inextricably locked
That the nuclear submarine had to be docked.
And into Pearl Harbor the *Swordfish* then went
Because of a paint scraper, fifty-four cent.

And out of the water on a big dry-dock lift,
One can see how the officers must have been miffed,
And the Pearl Harbor shipyard, its gear and its men,
Went to work on the *Swordfish*, repaired it, and then,
Went over the hull to prevent any leak,
And the whole operation took only a week.

All in all, quite expensive, you must understand.
It cost just about 171 grand.
And who was the fellow and what was his name
Whose slip of the mind was most likely to blame?
Of such people the brass take a view rather dim,
But they don't know who did it, and lucky for him.

Now, what sort of lesson has all of this taught?
That the price of a thing at the time that it's bought
Has little to do with the ultimate cost
If somebody goofs up and the battle is lost,
That the cheapest and simplest kind of a tool
Can cost a great deal in the hands of a fool.

I like the title *War and Peace*
It's better than *Peace and War*
Unfortunately, I am told,
It has been used before.

War and Peace

Anybody Wanna Buy a Goat?

Cars are made to go over roads. So six years ago, when the army decided it wanted to have a truck that would go over land where there are no roads, it didn't go to a car company. It went instead to an aerospace contractor that had no previous experience with trucks at all: Ling Temco Voight. LTV came up with an idea for a truck that the army thought was terrific. It was called the Gamma Goat.

The Gamma Goat would have not four wheels, but six. There would be two boxlike sections connected by a joint that gives— goes up when the terrain goes up, down when the terrain goes down. It would travel up to fifty-five miles an hour, would be amphibious, and you could drop it out of an airplane on a para- chute without hurting it *too* much. There were competitive bids to see who could produce the Gamma Goat, as designed by LTV, and LTV won.

That, as I said, was six years ago. Somewhere along the line the Gamma Goat project, which was supposed to cost $69 million, got to cost $439 million. And the Goat itself grew—from a little fellow hardly bigger than a jeep to a big old 7.5 tons, which is about as heavy a truck as the army has. The project also fell some- what behind schedule. First it was only a month or so behind. But then it got to be six months, and a year, and finally the Gamma Goat was three years late. Brigadier General Vincent Ellis, the army's procurement deputy, got to worrying about it, but recently reported that he was pleased with the results of what he calls his ramrodding of the Gamma Goat project.

Recently, Senator William Proxmire, whose Joint Economic Sub- committee gets involved in all kinds of cost-overrun controversies, had a hearing in which he told General Ellis, "I don't want to be unfair to you, but I am astonished that you were pleased with the Gamma Goat progress. You have got a program," the senator said to the general, "that is three years late. And you have a truck that is three times heavier than it was supposed to be and does not have a bigger payload—and one that is twice as expensive as the original estimate. It seems to me," said Proxmire, looking right into General Ellis's eye, "that you are an easy man to please."

The general protested that he was not an easy man to please. He said the estimate was only an estimate, that the doubled unit price had to be expected with something as newfangled as a Gamma Goat. He said, look at the maintenance, the Goat costs less to maintain than it was supposed to. Or rather, it is supposed to cost less than it was supposed to. It's hard to tell, since there have been no field tests of production-line samples.

The Gamma Goat is small potatoes as military cost overruns go. Peanuts compared to the TFX or the C5A. But, says Senator Proxmire, "it is one of the strangest cases ever to come before this committee."

Elmer Staats, the U.S. controller general, says it's a prominent example of buying something before you really know what you want.

Moral: The way Uncle spends his nieces' and nephews' money sometimes can really get your Gamma Goat.

The Ship-to-Drone Gap

DASH is an acronym. DASH stands for Drone Anti-Submarine Helicopter.

In 1959 the navy was really excited about the possibilities of a chopper that would fly without a pilot at the controls, would carry a torpedo, and, using a specially developed sonar system, would guide itself to an enemy submarine. And, in any kind of weather, day or night, would be able to attack the enemy without risking the life of a pilot. The navy was so excited, in fact, that they let contracts to develop the DASH drones and to build some of them.

The trouble seems to be that the contract to build and deliver the drones was carried out before the development contract was. And as a result, when $275 million had been spent, nothing very constructive had happened. Several destroyers were modified and adapted to launch and recover the DASHes. Unfortunately, the ships were ready long before the drones were.

Three years before, to be exact.

This is what the General Accounting Office is calling the ship-to-drone gap. Finally, after three years of having ships but no drones, along came the first DASH. The officers could hardly wait to try it out. They got it all ready, pushed the necessary buttons, and the ship sure enough took off all by itself. And flew nice as you please over the horizon. And disappeared. And nobody ever saw it again.

This is not the way it was supposed to happen. But, as additional DASH drones were launched from additional modified destroyers, it kept happening again and again. In fact, of the 750 DASHes accepted by the navy, the General Accounting Office says 362 of them disappeared in much the same way. Presumably to some unceremonious unintended ocean burial.

Congressman Sidney Yates of Illinois says actually 411 of the drones were lost. Anyway, sometime in 1966 the navy decided it better not buy any more of these things. And, in fact, hasn't bought any since, and has no plans to buy any more.

It is a pity that the sonar system wasn't better developed when the DASH was being tried out. However, technical problems cropped up, and the sonar was still on the drawing board when the DASHes were flying their one-way trips off destroyers. Later, though, the sonar was perfected, and the units were delivered to the fleet—roughly two years after the DASH program had been scrapped.

How did this all happen? GAO believes, according to a report put out by the agency, "The difficulties experienced with the system resulted in large part from the navy's ordering the drone helicopters into production before they were developed and tested."

Oh, I see.

The Nuclear Club Is an
Equal Opportunity Organization

The atom was a secret for a long time, known to none.
But the desert sun rose twice one day. And then there was one.
It was out there in New Mexico, and we were still at war.
And victory was wanted. That was what the bomb was for.
It was there to be discovered. Maybe nothing could have
    stopped it.
And as soon as it was tested, why, we went ahead and popped it.
It was terrible and frightening, yet we could be secure.
For only we would have the bomb. Of that we felt quite sure.
And we would never use it unless worse should come to worst.
And certainly, we told the world, we'd never use it first.

A nuclear monopoly is what this country knew
Until the Russians set one off. And then there were two.
The two of us proceeded then to run a mighty race,
With each determined not to find itself in second place.
We built and stored and tested and our arsenals improved.
We had to do it, we both said, necessity behooved.
It wasn't something one could leave to faith, much less to luck.
And so, we found out how to make a bigger bang per buck.
The world watched this titantic standoff, feeling rather skittish,
While some were working on their own, as did, of course, the
    British.

And the club expanded membership, for then there were three.
Already we began to think how awful it would be
If everybody had the bomb as easily as we.
We began to think of ways to limit who should join the group.
For if certain people had the bomb, we'd all be in the soup.
And the world was playing, so to speak, a nuclear roulette.
For they knew that it would come someday that someone else
    would get
The power that the three of us and only us then had.
And if any other country got it, why, that would be quite bad.

We even came to realize that it would sure be best
If even those of us who had it watched the way we test.
For the evidence was mounting, it was very clearly there,
That it did a lot of harm when you explode these in the air.
We'd been taking, we then realized, a very risky chance.
And in 1960, as it happened, came the turn of France.
It was in the South Pacific that it happened, what is more,
That the French exploded their device. And then there were four.
And the French refused to sign the test-ban treaty, for you see,
The French don't see why they can't be the same as you or me.
And if right out in the atmosphere is where we at one time tested,
The French will not allow themselves for a moment to be bested.

It was only four years later, much to add to our unease,
That another people joined the club, and they were the Chinese.
The Chinese set off their device and that way did arrive
In quite a growing company, for now there were five.
And who would be the next to join the ever-growing mix?
India has one, you know. And now there are six.
And who will be the seventh? Who will wear number eight?
Will it be Iran or Egypt, as these things proliferate?
Oh, the world has many people. But when all is said and done,
We had better watch our step, my friends, or soon there'll be
    none.

War Is Better Than Ever

The family of man was once at war
With the family that lived in the cave next door.
And they fought that way for many a year
'Til they learned to conquer hate and fear.
And teamed their forces that they might meet
The looming presence across the street.

And the looming presence became a war
That was even worse than the war before.
And they fought that way for many a year
'Til they learned to conquer hate and fear.
And combined their armies to go put down
The evil force from the other town.

With that evil force they fought a war
That was even worse than the war before.
And they fought that way for many a year
'Til they learned to conquer hate and fear.
And when it was done, they knelt to pray,
But some men worshiped a heathen way.

And religious difference became a war
That was even worse than the war before.
And they fought that way for many a year
'Til they learned to conquer hate and fear.
And built great navies that they might free
The captive peoples across the sea.

And with ships and guns they fought a war
That was even worse than the war before.
And they fought that way for many a year
'Til they learned to conquer hate and fear.
And nations prospered and empires, too,
And the size and scope of the conflicts grew.

And conflicting interests produced a war
That was even worse than the war before.

And they fought that way for many a year
'Til they learned to conquer hate and fear.
And built defenses to guard their shores,
And they fought a war to end all wars.

And the war they fought to end all war
Was even worse than the war before.
And they fought that way for many a year
'Til they learned to conquer hate and fear.
And they counted down, and they set the stage,
And they gave the world the Atomic Age.

And if there comes an atomic war
It will be far worse than the wars before.
There's an ancient, deadly pattern burned,
And the question is, has the family learned?
Or do we still pattern how we behave
After how it was in the family cave?

To everything there is a season,
There need not be a rhyme or reason.
Yet no matter what the time is,
Reason's much more scarce than rhyme is.

Seasons and Holidays

Good-bye Columbus, and Don't Come Back No More

In the year 1492
Columbus sailed the ocean blue.
This marvelous Italian fella
So impressed Queen Isabella
She underwrote the daring trip
And every crewman, every ship.
And what was really a mistake
Turned out quite a lucky break.

For Christopher believed at least
He'd find a shortcut to the East.
And in that respect he failed
As on and on and on he sailed.
Can you imagine, let us say,
The way it would work out today?
Through hypothetic eyes I've seen
That famous meeting with the queen.

Some receptionist, a dumbo
Who never heard of Chris Columbo
And therefore had no deference due,
Would ask, "What's it in reference to?"
And if he managed to get past her,
Possibly by running faster,
He'd find the royal person here
A telephone up to her ear.

"Have a seat," she'd say to Chris,
"Be with you when I've finished this."
And intercomming, modern style,
She'd tell her girl to bring the file
Of exploration lists to her
And on Columbus, Christopher.
From the folder comes a hint out—
A typical computer printout.

"Christopher," explains the queen,
"We've put your plan through the machine,
And through its real-time calculations
We've unearthed some perturbations.
First of all, can an Italian
Make it in a Spanish galleon?
As to ships, if you get any,
Three ships is two ships too many.

"East is east and west is west . . .
To get east sailing east is best.
Though no expert I claim to be,
That certainly makes sense to me.
Why bird hunt with a bird in hand?
(I got that line from Ferdinand)

"So to help you with your mission
We've appointed a commission
Just to study pro and con
Whether your trip is off or on.
Come back in a year or two
And we'll tell you what to do.

"Now, if you'll excuse me, Chris,
I hate to brush you off like this,
But plans this afternoon are made—
I'm witnessing a big parade.
What's the occasion, dare you say?
Why, silly, it's Columbus Day."

Christmas and Other Unlikely Events

The Salvation Army has a message this morning for whoever it was that took the big Christmas kettle from in front of Macy's department store in Manhattan. A prank is a prank, but please bring it back. Salvation Army brigadier Frank Gibson points out that the disappearance is itself a little miraculous. The red iron kettle, which has been there for the last twenty Christmas seasons, was five feet in diameter, three and a half feet high, and weighed three hundred pounds.

The Christmas season is getting off to an unorthodox start in a lot of places, it seems. The Holiday Photo and Display Company of Chicago says it was justified in not hiring Cynthia Larson, who has filed a sex discrimination complaint against the company. Miss Larson, who is nineteen, had applied for the job of Santa Claus. Company president Robert Heiss says that the two men hired for the job were more of the boisterous Ho Ho Ho types people expect Santa Claus to be. Miss Larson was hired as a Santa's helper, but filed the complaint anyway, maintaining that in order to go Ho Ho Ho you don't have to be a he he he.

There's an assortment of strange little stories this morning. In San Raphael, California, Walter Harper has been arraigned on charges of ripping the telephone receivers out of public phone booths. Harper told the sheriff's deputies he's been vandalizing phone booths ever since his wife ran off with an employee of the phone company.

Jack Teehan of the Social Resources office of Honolulu City County got a letter yesterday from American Express—a two-page letter signed by the president of the Credit Card Division and enclosing a credit card application blank. It was addressed to Mr. Honolulu City County, and it started out, "Dear Mr. County."

The state of West Virginia has gone into the moonshine business. The state Alcoholic Beverage Commission, noting that some people seem to like white lightning better than the more aged stuff, are stocking Georgia Moon and Boonshine, two brands of corn whiskey, which the state says are "guaranteed to be less than thirty days old."

In Michigan, inmate George Nawrocki of Southern Michigan

Prison in Jackson has filed suit to allow prisoners to wear long hair, goatees, beards, and moustaches. It's a discrimination suit. Women prisoners have no such regulations to contend with, Nawrocki says. The case is assigned to Judge Cornelia Kennedy.

Not everybody is dissatisfied these days. The commander of the U.S. Air Force Phantomjet Squadron, Alconbury Royal Air Force Base, says in a notice to his men, "I'm glad I am in England. The natives are friendly, and the language is quite similar to ours."

And finally this morning, a fascinating statistic from the National Council on Crime and Delinquency, which says that the best parole risks are convicted murderers. A study of the records of 6,903 paroled killers compared with 72,192 other prisoners shows that over 9 percent of the other offenders ended up back in jail, but less that 2 percent of murderers did. That may not tell as much about convicted murderers as it does about statistics.

What politics is all about
Is being in or being out.
The Ins have power on their side.
They almost always point with pride.
While viewing with alarm, the Outs
Express their fears and gravest doubts.
The Ins fall out, the Outs are Ins.
And once again it all begins.

Politics and Bureaucracy

La Forza del Bologna

Law enforcement in Italy has been criticized of late by some, who feel that the authorities there have not cracked down severely enough on those who break the law. Now from Rome comes the reassuring news that the police have arrested twenty-nine people, including some of the biggest names in Italian opera. In a scene worthy of a Verdi spectacular, Prince Giocchino Lanza Tomasi of the Rome Opera House, Francesco Siciliano of La Scala, Adriano Falvo of San Carlo, and many other very important people in the opera world were arrested. Singer/agent Simonetta Lippi and conductor Claudio Abbado face currency violation charges. Most of the others are charged with taking kickbacks from singers in exchange for operatic roles. In fact, it seems to me if Giuseppi Verdi were alive today, he might well ask Arrigo Boito to turn out a libretto, and the world might have yet another operatic masterpiece titled (let us say) *La Forza del Bologna*.

La Forza del Bologna by Verdi is set in Italy, three-quarters of the way through the twentieth century. It is a time of trouble and uncertainty, with political terrorism rampant and fear in the streets. The overture begins with an ominous chord followed by the theme of the main chorus, the haunting, *"Non ci telefonare, telefoniamono noi,"* which, roughly translated, means, "Don't call us, we'll call you." The first-act curtain rises on a happy scene: The townspeople are gathered in a local dancing establishment or "disco," as it is called, and are gaily thrashing about to a lively peasant quadrille entitled *"Il Febbre di Sabato Sera,"* which all seem to know well and which is sung at an extremely high decibel level by a trio of townspeople known as "Bee Gees." We meet one young man, Don Travolta, whose dancing is especially brilliant and whose ambition is to sing in the great opera house at La Scala in Milan. We learn in a recitative that Don Travolta has an appointment the very next day with a top man at the opera, one Principio Giovanni. And Travolta sings of his dreams in the tenor aria *"Stare con me, mia bambina,"* which means, roughly, "Stick with me, baby." And the curtain falls.

In act two, Don Travolta is off to Milan for his audition. And his girl friend, Donna Karen, encourages him and eggs him on with her touching description of how much her life will be changed when he becomes an opera star. The lyric soprano aria: *"I diamanti sono il migliore amico d'una ragazza,"* meaning literally, "Diamonds are a girl's best friend."

Don Travolta's audition is a smashing success. And Il Principio offers him a job, introducing himself as Travolta's new boss. *"Mi chiamano bossa nuova,"* he sings, explaining that if Don Travolta expects any decent roles in the opera, he's going to have to cough up a little kickback out of his pay, which will be substantial if he plays his cards right. Principio, the bass baritone, then delivers the unforgettable solo, *"Ha ha ha, il tuo denaro, e il mio denaro"* ("Your money is my money"), which includes the famous Mephistophelian laugh sequence. Travolta, unamused, blows the whistle in the amusing whistle scene, featuring the chorus dressed in the colorful costumes of the Italian fiscal police.

In the third act comes the grand finale, in which twenty-nine leading figures in the world of Italian opera are brought onstage in handcuffs, as Don Travolta and Donna Karen, bedecked in diamonds, stand by approvingly, and the chorus sings the rousing *"No che un business come show business"* as the final curtain falls on *La Forza del Bologna.*

Political Boxing

Politics can be kind of interesting sometimes. Especially in Philadelphia, where recently plainclothes policemen had to pull two
politicians apart in the city council after one of them called the
other a faggot and the second one called the first one a racist.
And the first one challenged the second one to a boxing match,
and the second one accepted, and a fight promoter suggested a
date and a place: August 24 at the Spectrum.

It's not customary for us to report on boxing matches here
on this broadcast. We are a peace-loving, order-loving, nonviolent
sort of broadcast, not given to extensive coverage of small-time
fisticuffs. However, we are prepared to make an exception. For on
the card at the Spectrum in Philadelphia on the night of August
24, promoter J. Russell Peltz wants to feature, along with middle-
weights Benny Briscoe and Marvin Hagler, a couple of heavy-
weights named Francis Rafferty and Milton Street.

Street is thirty-seven years old. Rafferty is forty. Street weighs
in at 210 pounds. Rafferty at 190. Rafferty is a member of the
Philadelphia City Council. Street is Democratic candidate for the
181st district of the Pennsylvania State Legislature. Rafferty used
to be an amateur boxer. He fought fifteen welterweight bouts in
the army and after his discharge. Street has fought in the streets,
but never in a fight ring before. He has suffered in the past from
multiple sclerosis, but he says that's strictly in the past. His mus-
cles are under control now, he says. Street became a street ven-
dor after his illness and made himself famous in Philly by organizing black street vendors into a lobbying force. Last summer
he moved poor people into some federally owned abandoned
houses, and that got him some national attention.

Well, this week in the city council there was a hearing on
whether to change the city charter so that Mayor Frank Rizzo
could run for a third time (which he would like to do). Rafferty,
a Rizzo supporter, would like him to do it. But Street, who is not
a Rizzo supporter, would not like him to do it. So Rafferty argued
for changing the charter, and Street argued against it. The argu-
ment grew heated—to say the least. Rafferty called Street a faggot. Street called Rafferty a racist. Plainclothes police had to pull

them apart. And afterward, Rafferty said, "You name your favorite charity. I'll get a match with Milton Street at the Spectrum."

When Street was told about it, he said, "Tell Rafferty he's on. Bad health and all, I'll take him on."

Now promoter Peltz, recognizing a good draw when he sees one, stepped right in. There'd be no problem, he said, getting the approval of the Pennsylvania State Athletic Commission. Howard McCall is the chairman of that commission, and so far he's not been available for comment. But Leon Katz is appalled. Katz is the chancellor-elect of the Philadelphia Bar Association, and he's dead set against the Street-Rafferty boxing match.

"It would set a dreadful example and make our city the laughingstock of the country," he says.

As an example, of course, it does suggest a new forum for the resolving of political differences. Whether the issues would be lost in the left jabs and right crosses and fancy footwork, it's hard to say. But politicians on all levels are prone to displays of fancy footwork as it is.

But as we say, politics sure can be interesting.

The Hatfields Were the Real McCoy

Old Paul Hatfield made it to San Diego from up in Pear Blossom 'cause he wanted to see that collection of his late brother Charlie's stuff they're showing at the main San Diego Library.

Might have been a few people worried Paul might try to collect the ten thousand dollars he says the city owes him and Charlie, Lord rest his soul. They had that money coming since 1916. You figure it out what that's worth now—ten thousand dollars at compound interest for fifty-six years. Now that would amount to something! But no, Paul Hatfield didn't go back to San Diego at the age of eighty-five to collect or make trouble for anybody. Just wanted to see the exhibit down at the library and bring along some more gear of Charlie's maybe people didn't know about.

Charlie's barometer, his scale, his rain gauge.

Charlie Hatfield was a rainmaker. A moisture accumulator is what he called himself. For thirty years he made a career out of it. And without a doubt, his most spectacular performance was the one San Diego refused to pay him for in 1916. That was the year they had this awful drought, and the farmers were worried sick, and the Morena Reservoir was all but dry. The deal was, Charlie worked it out, ten thousand dollars payable when the reservoir was full up. Town figured what did it have to lose? If the Hatfields didn't produce the rain—18 billion gallons or something—in the Morena Reservoir inside of one year, why, the city didn't have to pay. Couldn't lose. Or so the city councilmen figured.

So Paul and Charlie Hatfield went to work. They set up their twenty-four-foot log tower right there by the reservoir, a few miles out of town. Charlie mixed up a few batches of his secret moisture-accumulator formula, and the boys set it out in pans. That was January the fifth, 1916.

San Diego gave them 'til January the fifth, 1917, to fill that reservoir. But they didn't have to wait that long, because ten days later it started to rain. And it rained and rained and rained. And in twenty-seven days the reservoir was full, but the rain didn't stop. It kept raining until 110 of the 112 bridges in the county were washed away. Communication lines were knocked out. Orchards were ruined. A few miles south of Morena the dam burst at Otay, and water came roaring down the canyon. Homes were swept away. Twenty people died in the floods.

Now everybody was after Paul and Charlie to make the rain stop. But they never had claimed they knew how to do that. They delivered the rain, and now they wanted their money. The San Diego city councilmen huddled and came to the conclusion that the Hatfields did not cause the rain. It must have been caused by something else.

Because if Charlie and Paul were what made it rain, then the city council was also responsible, and maybe liable, for all the damage that the water had done. No two ways about it. If they paid the moisture accumulators their ten thousand dollars, they'd open themselves wide to lawsuits in the millions. Sorry, Charlie. Sorry, Paul.

So the boys went away empty-handed, assured by the kind gentlemen they were better off washing their hands of the whole thing. People might sue the Hatfields, too, if they admitted they'd done it . . . by taking the ten thousand . . . don't you see?

"We did it. No question about that," said Paul the other day.

Charlie died fourteen years ago at the age of eighty-three. Paul? He just stopped in a few minutes at the library and headed out of town. Doesn't like to stay in San Diego any more'n he has to. Headed right back to Pear Blossom. Nice little town, Pear Blossom. Annual rainfall a steady six inches a year.

Can She Bake a Cherry Pie, Billy Boy, Billy Boy—and Does It Meet the Federal Cherry Pie Specifications?

It could very well be that you're wondering why
There should be any trouble about cherry pie.
Cherry pie has been something that people just ate
Without any conflict or heated debate.

Why should anyone argue, get angry, or scream?
You just eat it
With maybe a scoop of ice cream.

But the folks in the government's own FDA
Don't let anything get quite that simple today.

And so what they've done for the last seven years
Is to turn their attention and gear up their gears
To setting some standards with which to comply
When making a frozen-to-sell cherry pie.

It was in '66 that the issue arose,
When some cherry pie makers complained that their toes
Had been stepped on by some of their own competition,
Who, by a process of greed or attrition,
Had scrimped in their pies in their use of the cherry,
Which these makers regarded as terrible—very!

They wanted the government to specify
Some fixed numbers of cherries in such cherry pie.
But a lesson these pie makers then had to learn
That the wheels that the government once made to turn
Are harder to stop than they were to make go.
And they turn, do those wheels, most incredibly slow.

So the FDA took to examining pies,
To studying all of the whats and the whys.

They weighed and they counted, they measured and tasted,
Defined and refined. Not a moment they wasted.

They checked out diameter, depth of the pans,
And compared this man's sweetness to that other man's.
They found out that left out for sake of expedience
Were some of the rather more basic ingredients.

Harold Saulwin, a fellow who's one of the dudes
Who works at the FDA's Bureau of Foods,
Says the cherry pie matter would not go away.
And he's happy they've got it resolved now today.

For the cherry pie recipe you use, you see,
May be quite a bit different than that used by me.
And some pie makers just couldn't understand why
They should have to revise how they make cherry pie.

Well, they started out promising they'd be cooperative
That turned out to be, as we now say, inoperative.

Setting standards, it's hard to know where one should start.
Some folks like their pie sweeter, but some like it tart.
Why should Uncle Sam spend any good time and money
Counting cherries in pies?
Oh, it seems a bit funny.

But unless you have standards, about what you call
A cherry pie, it might have no cherries at all.
Some makers insist, they will freely confess,
That they use fewer cherries, so they can charge less.

The bureau would make its suggestions, of course,
Which they just weren't able at all to enforce.
And the bureaucrats were worn down to a tissue,
Deciding this delicate cherry pie issue.

They wanted to set certain standard parameters
For their cherries, in pie pans of different diameters.

164

The compounding factor that caused them to weep
Was the varying thickness—how shallow or deep.

And not all pies are round, as if anyone cared.
I'm sure you'll remember that some "pie" are squared.

Well, the upshot is this: They decided to make,
As a standard for such pies a baker may bake,
Cherries must make up one-fourth of the weight.
And the new regulation goes on then to state
That no more than a figure of 15 percent
Of the cherries involved can be blemished or bent.

The rules take effect at the end of the year,
After which you can feast without wonder or fear
That perhaps you're not getting your quota of cherries
Or that someone has introduced substitute berries.

Seven years it has been. How the time has just flown!
'Til the end of the year, then, you're still on your own.

Rock Watching

If you are a contemplative sort with a lot of inner resources, I have the perfect job for you: rock watcher.

I am indebted to the Sturgeses, Frederick and Margaret, in Orange, Connecticut, who perceived in a recent New York City news story the possibilities for a terrific new way of making a living: rock watching.

The city Transit Authority is going to be digging up part of Central Park to build a tunnel for a new subway. It is going to take quite a while, and things will be a mess, of course, while it's going on. But the Parks Commission agreed to it. Agreed to it for several reasons, and with several qualifications. For one thing the subway people promised to put everything right back the way it was before the digging started. There'd even be some improvements—better playgrounds and such. But except for those, they said, every rock could be put back in place, and the Parks Department will see to it that this is, in fact, done.

That's where the rock watchers come in. You need a rock watcher to notice where each rock is to start with, what is happening to it during the years of construction, and to show the workmen where to put the rock when they are done.

Rock watching is not a job for a man or woman easily bored. But because of the grave threat of boredom, the job will no doubt be highly paid. Furthermore, one cannot be expected to watch rocks incessantly without a break, so there would have to be some sort of rock-watching schedule worked out, with deputy rock watchers to fill in and help. And of course a night rock watcher would be entitled to a special night rock-watching differential. Before you apply, however, you will want to look into such matters as fringe benefits—retirement and all that. Young rock watchers may pooh-pooh this, but as the years go on, there comes a time when one doesn't watch rocks with the enthusiasm one once did. And what's a rock watcher to do then, unless his union has worked out a good pension plan? Oh yes, there will have to be a union to fight for better working conditions. Perhaps a local of the International Brotherhood of Featherbedders, Goldbrickers, and Rock Watchers could be set up to hear grievances and be a bargaining agent.

There's the matter of job security to think about, too. Once the Central Park project is through, many, many years from now, will they just let all those experienced rock watchers go? Or will they have it in their contracts that they'll be assigned to other projects—star gazing for NASA, or pipe dreaming for the Department of the Interior, or wool gathering for the Department of Agriculture.

If you wish to apply, please be sure to list your rock experience—watching, that is (throwing doesn't count). You may be embarking on an exciting new career.

Apt. Avl. Quiet St. No Wtr.

One day two years ago, Mardig Kachian turned on the water tap and nothing came out. They had turned the water off on him. They being New York City—his landlord.

Mardig Kachian is a sculptor who lives alone in an apartment and studio at 179 West Street in lower Manhattan. When I say alone, I mean alone. Not only does nobody else live with him in the four rooms on the second floor, with studio on the third floor, but nobody else lives in the whole building. In fact, he has about the whole street to himself. One by one tenants have moved out; one by one buildings have been torn down to make way for the Washington Street Urban Renewal Project (whatever that is). And they tried to move Kachian out, too. But he wouldn't. Where else was he going to get all that for seveny-five dollars a month? And besides, he'd been there a long time—since 1960.

No sir, he didn't want to move out. So he didn't.

After the water got shut off that day, Kachian ran a garden hose from a fire hydrant. That was not too handy, but it was all right. Until the city shut the hydrant off, too. Somebody up there didn't like him and was giving him these gentle hints that maybe he should split.

But the sculptor thought that was unreasonable. After all, the city didn't know yet what it was going to do in this urban renewal area. Plans hadn't been finalized. So why the big hurry to tear the building down? That was what he asked his lawyer, and that is what his lawyer asked the relocation people. And getting no satisfactory answer, the lawyer brought suit on behalf of Kachian. (In the meantime Kachian had been bringing water into the apartment by pail.)

Last month a federal judge ruled that the building should stand until the city makes up its mind what the renewal plan is going to be. And now a state judge has ruled that the city has to turn Kachian's water back on. But, said the city lawyers, to do that a hole would have to be drilled in the street above the water main and connected to the line running to the building and then the street would have to be refilled and repaved. All of which would take at least two weeks, and a lot of work and a lot of money.

Said the judge, State Supreme Court Justice James Leff, "Any expense imposed on the city in restoring the water supply is a consequence of its own conduct." That's judicialese for, You made your bed, now lie in it.

And so, in the eternal struggle of the little guy against the big city, chalk one up for the little guy.

Invented Here

After man had evolved from the primal slime,
He got along for a good long time
Without using much energy—not much at all.
For gas and oil, he had little call.
He discovered fire, that was nice
For keeping warm and melting ice.
And his biggest discovery, some still feel,
Was when he invented, or found, the wheel.

He trained the wind, which was there for free,
To push his boats across the sea.
And now and then when the wind would fail,
There was no breeze to fill his sail,
He'd lean on the oars to control his fate.
But outside of that, he could only wait.

And on land, what he learned to tame, of course,
Was a strong, speedy animal called the horse.
No roaring engine, no carbon haze,
They used real horsepower in those old days.
For centuries, that's how it went.
Only recently did man invent
The countless machines and assorted devices
That have led us now to the energy crisis.

It was when the Americans came along,
With minds creative and genius strong,
That many wonderful ways were found
To tap the energy in the ground.
It was men with vision and boundless dreams
Who great inventions produced, it seems.
A bold new future—a kind of birth—
And changed the face of the planet Earth.

Robert Fulton had a dream—
To make a boat that would run on steam.

"Fulton's Folly," the people said,
But a dream still flourished in Fulton's head.
McCormick, and Eli Whitney, too,
Showed what technology could do.
In planting, harvesting, treating crops—
The wonder of it never stops.

And a greater wonder you will not find
Than Thomas Edison's fertile mind.
And the bicycle makers—the brothers Wright—
Who brought mankind to the age of flight.
And Henry Ford and his Model T
Gave ideas to others of what might be.
And on and on as the time unfurled
American ideas changed the world.

And other nations learned they could do
What we did and have what we have, too.
But that is a most elusive goal—
For it takes oil and gas and coal.
And supplies of all that useful stuff
Are running out—there is not enough.
Our need for energy has grown
Too much, too fast, if the truth be known.
We must change our ways, for it's plain to see
That the future's not what it used to be.
We must find new ways, we must find new sources—
As once we turned from the wind and horses.

And so now that we are in a bind,
Again, the answer is in the mind.
And who is likely to solve the riddle
Of which we now are in the middle?
America must, and must do it soon,
We who've walked on the far-off moon.
From Land, to Watson, to Jonas Salk,
American know-how is not just talk.
We've got a major problem—there is no doubt.
We've thought our way in, we must think our way out.

171

The energy crisis, it's fair to say,
Was manufactured in the U.S.A.

But as sure as Fulton and Ford were told
That their ideas could not be sold,
As sure as the Wrights were told to stop
And go back to Dayton and their bicycle shop.
There will be those who will no doubt say,
When it comes to the energy crunch today:
"Don't look for answers, for there are none,
Don't waste your time, for it can't be done."

The El Cajon Story

When you are a bureaucrat, there's very little thanks
For making up the many forms, for filling in the blanks,
That contain the needed data for the agencies to file,
Or stack upon each other in a neat and dandy pile.
But you have to have the paperwork to keep the process going.
To feed the need for rules to heed, the paperwork keeps flowing.
The story that we tell today by no means stands alone;
It has to do with something that occurred in El Cajon.

It could have happened anywhere, that we have to warn you,
Although in this instance it occurred in California.
El Cajon's a city, an officer of which
Is the personnel administrator, a fellow name of Fitch.
John Fitch could see no reason and could perceive no harm,
In allowing Uncle Sam to pay for burglar alarms—
Money from the government absolutely free,
Derived, of course, from taxpayers like him and you and me—
A program that's administered all throughout the nation
By the Federal Law Enforcement Assistance Administration.

El Cajon was eligible, so the lawyer stated,
On the basis of its size and needs, the city rated
Money back for money spent already out of hand,
Eight thousand dollars' worth. The city sure could use eight grand.
Such was the logic at the time, such was the thinking which
Led the Personnel Department and its officer, John Fitch,
To start the wheels to turning so that Washington would send
The money back to El Cajon on other things to spend.

Sounds simple, I am sure, and so it sounded then to Fitch.
Eight thousand bucks is not enough to make the city rich,
But it would help to put some coins into the city's purse
If what they'd spent on those alarms Uncle Sam would reimburse.
So Fitch sent a note of inquiry, thus touching off the storms,
The lightning and the thunder and the heavy rain of forms.

There were forms enough to curl your hair and cause your teeth
     to ache:
Forms for the equipment and each model, year, and make.
Forms about the city in the smallest detail known,
About the population and the thieves of El Cajon.
Forms to show compliance with a thousand laws and rules,
About the cops of El Cajon, the firemen, the schools.
Forms that dealt with civil rights and equal opportunity,
With blanks that could not be ignored, at least not with
     impunity.

When Fitch saw what he'd have to do to get the town the money,
He was not the least amused, he did not find it funny.
In the labor it would take to get the paperwork completed,
The cost involved would be so great the purpose was defeated.
What use in getting such a grant, John Fitch sadly said,
If the money we get back we're spending getting it instead?
Why go to all the bother and the labor costs and such
If to get the funds from Washington costs every bit as much?

Free money from the government sounds very, very nice,
But El Cajon has learned that, though it's free, it has its price.
Two hundred man-hours it would cost, should they decide to
     let it;
So Fitch wrote back to Washington and told them to forget it.
The forms remain unfilled, and nothing's written in the blanks,
And El Cajon has, in effect, said thank you, but no thanks!

The Randall's Island Principle

Head waiters, movie ushers, hotel clerks, receptionists, and government clerks may seem to be there for the obvious reasons—to help you to do something. But experience shows that this is, in fact, untrue. Often they are there to make sure you do not do whatever it is you have in mind.

I first discovered the Randall's Island Principle on Randall's Island, where the city of New York maintains several tennis courts. In theory, the tennis courts are to play tennis on, and the men who attend the tennis courts are, in theory, there to help people *do* that. But, in fact, they appear to do all they can to make sure you do not play tennis.

One sunny day the truth of it came to me in a blinding flash. All the gates were locked, save one—the one most distant from the parking lot. There was a sign up, NO TENNIS TODAY—WET GROUNDS, though it had not rained since the day before, and if anything, the courts were dusty. It turned out the sign was there from yesterday, just a decoy to turn away as many of the unsuspecting as possible. The attendant looked us over, and though we were attired in whites, and carried tennis rackets and a can of balls, he asked us what he could do for us. When we explained our mission, he asked to see our permits. I had one, but my friend had some trouble finding his, and during the search the attendant made it clear that it looked as if I could play—but I would have to play alone.

Not too satisfactory, that, but my opponent found his permit and we were about to go on the court when the attendant thought of something. "Let me see the bottoms of your shoes," he said. Mine passed inspection. My partner's did not. Wrong kind of tread. The attendant was not to be dissuaded.

All those courts—eighteen of them, I believe—and not a soul playing as we trudged our way to the parking lot. It was then the realization hit: the Randall's Island Principle.

There on the smiling face of the tennis attendant was the look I had seen on so many head waiters who had told me (though dozens of empty tables could be seen) that there would be a short wait. Or the hotel clerk who would not give a room to a real live customer because he has to save some rooms in case there are telephone reservations. (I know somebody who once went across the lobby and called the hotel from a phone booth and made a reservation.)

Have you ever tried to have your driver's license renewed? Motor Vehicle offices across the nation are staffed with skilled practitioners of the Randall's Island Principle.

The ostensible purpose of a receptionist is to receive you when you walk into an office. But her real purpose is to keep you from seeing anybody who doesn't want to be seen.

Personnel offices exist to keep you from trying to see somebody who might hire you.

Information offices frequently exist to make sure no information gets out. And so it goes.

The next time a taxi driver tries to interview you about where you're going . . . the next time the supermarket line gets ridiculously long and they still refuse to open another register . . . just remember, it is not your paranoia acting up. The world *is* fighting you.

Chalk it up to the Randall's Island Principle.

Sowa Long, It's Been Good to Know Ya

Politically, it isn't wise when friends feel they've been slighted.
So when you can, you try to see such people get invited.
A White House dinner, such as held for Nicolae Ceausescu,
Is a chance to make amends and do a social rescue.
And that's why dining there this week on royal squab and melon
Was Robert Sowa, used car dealer and convicted felon.

Many, many months ago it happened way back when.
And not too many people knew of Jimmy Carter then.
To the state they call New Hampshire did Mr. Carter go
To run in that state's primary and slosh through that state's snow.
It was in the course of doing that in the winter of '76
That Robert Sowa came along to certain problems fix.

He even threw a party to which Jimmy Carter came,
Since getting him acquainted was a big part of the game.
And there, where snow was flying and where winter winds did
    howl,
Sowa loaned galoshes to an aide named Jody Powell—
Kindnesses that might pay off should Carter be elected,
A likelihood that at the time not many folks suspected.

But sure enough, what people thought unlikely to be done
Is now spelled out in history—for Mr. Carter won.
And only this past February, and at the White House, too,
For New Hampshire's Democrats who helped the president get
    through,
There was a little party, and the thank-you's flew about,
But Robert Sowa wasn't there; he'd somehow been left out.

It made him quite unhappy to miss this social treat,
The man who'd put galoshes onto Jody Powell's feet.
And someone at the White House when he heard that this was
    true
Tried to make it up to Sowa. It seemed the thing to do.
And so it was this very week he sat among the great
At a dinner at the White House for a foreign chief of state.

Nicolae Ceausescu holds Rumania's top job,
And with him Sowa dined on a supreme of royal squab.
The guest list listed Sowa as New Hampshire representative,
But had they known the truth, they might have been a bit more
    tentative.
An alderman in Manchester he might have been depicted,
Except he'd been removed from that because he'd been convicted,

Had entered in a guilty plea to an insurance fraud,
Activity the White House cannot sanction nor applaud.
It seems that Robert Sowa, who was in the used car biz,
Made a claim that someone stole a car that had been his,
In order that he be relieved of some financial jams,
And collected from the company a cool three thousand clams.

He was fined a thousand dollars. Had to give the three grand
    back.
And for two years on probation must keep straight and on the
    track.
What he did's illegal in New York and Pennsylvania,
And is frowned on, one imagines, even over in Rumania.
He is not the sort of fellow that they'd send an invite to,
But the ones who did the sending hadn't heard and never knew.

Acquainted though they may have been with kings and movie
    stars,
What do they know of someone whose domain is used cars?
But somebody who saw the name, as someone always does,
Investigated to find out who Robert Sowa was.
An embarrassed White House employee, a lesson has been taught,
And now he knows that Sowa wasn't really what they thought.

The moral is for presidents, when you become the winner,
You've got to be a little careful whom you have for dinner.

A statue is a monument
To give someone a boost,
And grateful are the pigeons,
For they have someplace to roost.

Man and His Monuments

José, Can You See?

In Ecuador, in Guayaquil,
I'll tell you how the people feel
About José Olmedo, poet:
They're proud and want for you to know it.

There's a statue you'll find there today
That honors Guayaquil's José,
Erected with the gratitude
And reverential attitude
Of those who live in Guayaquil,
To whom he had a great appeal.
But if you sat beneath that statue
Looking up as there you sat, you
Might observe the statue tall
Looks nothing like José at all.

That's not his forehead, not his nose;
There's something wrong from head to toes.
That's not his hat upon the head;
It's someone else's hat instead.
Although the statue has a plaque
That has his name both front and back,
The figure standing in that place
Does not have Señor José's face.

There is a reason, you may guess,
There is, indeed, a reason, yes,
And it is more than just a whim;
Indeed, the statue isn't him.
In Ecuador, in Guayaquil,
The people, many of them, feel
That what was done down on the square,
The José Olmedo statue there,
Is not quite fair, not quite right;
They just may tear it down some night.

For at the base, the plaque does say,
Señor Olmedo's son, José,
A poet who expressed in rhymes
The feeling of his life and times
And won the pride, respect, and love
Of those he wrote his poems of.

The people that he wrote them for,
The common folk of Ecuador,
Were deeply moved, and when he died,
They all felt really bad and cried,
And someone said, "What we should do
Is build a statue fine and new.
José Olmedo, he's our poet,
And we want the world to know it.
Let's commission someone good
To sculpt José as best he could.
Everyone this would be good for,
Reminding us of what he stood for."

So, in a sense, he'd not be lost,
But that's before they knew the cost.
A sculptor who is worth his salt
Must charge a lot; it's not his fault.
It's just that such a thing takes time,
A whole lot longer than a rhyme.
A sculptor works with clay or stone
And has expenses of his own.
He needs a roof; he's got to eat;
When it gets cold, he needs some heat.
He needs materials and tools,
And those who sell them are not fools.
They want their money, want their pay,
And that's José or no José,

And so the price, when it was stated,
Was more than was anticipated.
Inflation, as you'd think it might,
Ate up another healthy bite,

As things were costing more and more
For folks who lived in Ecuador.
They decided they were in a mess,
That less is more and more is less.

They thought José would understand,
He who knew so well their land.
Poets are not rich, you know it,
Hence the expression "starving poet."
So what they did, their faith to keep,
Was buy a statue rather cheap
Of one George Gordon, called Lord Byron,
Instead of goin' out and hirin'
Someone who would start from scratch
To make José Olmedo's statch,
Lord Byron, he who wrote *Don Juan*,
Not a modern, shiny new one,
A statue old and secondhand
Of someone from another land.
A poet, oh, yes, to be sure,
But since the treasury was poor,
A poet not from Ecuador,
Who died in 1824.

And therefore, who is left to say,
"That's old Lord Byron, not José"?
The image new they did not make,
But who's to know, for goodness sake?
A poet's statue seeming real
Stands today in Guayaquil.
Olmedo, no—Lord Byron, yes—
The pigeons there could not care less.

The Salt of the Earth

Claridge's, in London town, an elegant hotel,
Is known for doing everything magnificently well.
From the moment you arrive there in your chauffeured limousine,
You enjoy the best of everything, from service to cuisine.
No wonder, then, the powerful, the mighty, and the rich
Prefer to stay at Claridge's and do not like to switch.
But something quite discomforting is now occurring there,
Suggesting that perhaps the winds of change are in the air.
A hundred twenty workers, kitchen helpers, and the like
Are picketing at Claridge's because they are on strike.

A strike is on at Claridge's in good old London town,
A bit of inconvenience, though they have not shut it down.
The hotel's coping nicely, a Claridge spokesman said,
Although we've heard a guest or two has had to make up his own
    bed.
They've drawn the line, it would appear, in this unseemly tiff,
The hotel has its upper lip appropriately stiff.
It's rather a depressing thing, of that there is no doubt,
Perhaps you will agree when you have heard what it's about.

It seems a chef's assistant, Robert Elvidge is his name,
Who's all of nineteen years old, is really who's to blame.
And what he did, this Elvidge chap, what makes him so at fault,
Was that in his ratatouille, he put insufficient salt.
Now the standards there at Claridge's are very, very high,
And insufficient salt is a sufficient reason why,
In the view of Claridge management, which wants to keep it so,
This Elvidge fellow would not do, and simply had to go.

We do not want a chef's assistant working here now, do we,
Who failed to put the right amount of salt in ratatouille?
So goes the line of management, its explanatory reasoning,
But it's more than just a matter of some ratatouille seasoning.
Young Elvidge did another thing they say got on their nerves,
He bothered the young lady there who made up the hors
    d'oeuvres.

Exactly how he bothered her, they don't precisely say,
But if one wants to speculate, then I suppose one may.
Many things would interfere, one might safely say,
With a girl who's stuffing anchovies or spreading a pâté,
And furthermore, the hotel says, it bothered them when he
Would stay there in the kitchen when he paused to take his tea.

So it all adds up to someone that they wish to be without.
And that's what caused the workers' strike,
And what it's all about.
But Elvidge, he of too light hand in salting ratatouille,
Says all of this is nonsense,
His response to them is "phooey."
What they don't take a fancy to, young Robert Elvidge claims,
"Is my organizing efforts," and that's what Elvidge blames.
To hear him tell the story, and he's not afraid to speak,
It's the fact that workers there now average fifty bucks a week,
And don't get to eat the fancy food, the elegant cuisine,
But have to eat whatever's in the employees' canteen.
It's over matters such as that that workers do not like,
That Elvidge says they're protesting with Claridge's first strike.
Rare would be the person who critically disparages,
The policies that bring about a place as fine as Claridge's.
Uncompromising quality is a lost art now, one fears,
Too bad, when an example of it fades or disappears.
Yet, wonderful as it may be to eat at or to visit,
To tell the truth it isn't where you'd want to work, now is it?

Sounds of the Earth

If there's life in the universe, out there in space,
Intelligent life in some faraway place,
And if you were to send them some things from our planet,
What would you send them and how would you plan it?

We're sending a package this summer, you know,
The Voyager spacecraft. And where will they go?
Past Jupiter, Saturn, our own little pond,
Uranus, and Neptune, and even beyond . . .

Out of the system controlled by our sun,
Where man's exploration has only begun.
And what will they carry in case they are found?
They may carry recordings. Recordings of sound.

Sounds of the Earth is a Carl Sagan dream
And NASA is giving it thought, it would seem.
They'd send up two records, it's now being said,
With instructions, a needle, and phonograph head.

And if Voyager's package should ever be found,
There would be these recordings of Earth and its sound.
If it's thought that the trouble is worth all the risks,
They'll include these two silvery phonograph discs

Of sounds to be heard by some far distant ear,
Recordings of us and of what we have here,
Hoping somehow that in fine grooves of steel
We can capture the sense of what we know and feel.

Better than drawings, some think that this plan
Communicates more about Earth, about man.
And if they approve the idea in the end,
These are some of the sounds Sagan thinks we should send:

The sound of the surf as it pounds on the shore,
To tell of the sea and the land, what is more.

And intelligent creatures might learn from those sounds
Of the rhythm of Earth, of the surf as it pounds.

The sound of the wind ought to cause them to wonder.
The patter of raindrops, the booming of thunder . . .
Perhaps to be heard not for millions of years
By some faraway galaxy's creatures' ears.

Sounds of our animals, songs of our birds,
And even our own sounds—some human with words.
"To whomever, wherever, may be concerned . . ."
There are certain things, we suppose, to be learned.

Hearing greetings in fifty or more of man's tongues,
They might gather that we have our mouths and our lungs.
But also, if ever that record they find,
Perhaps they'll discover our Earth creatures' minds.

We'll, of course, keep it simple, and you can see why.
Fifty Earth languages just to say "Hi!"
I don't see it mentioned, but please, NASA, please,
Include on your intergalactic LPs
The sound of our music. Please give them a song.
To not put in music would surely be wrong.
Without Bach or Mozart, the picture's not whole.
You'd give them our minds—would you leave out our soul?

One thing, incidentally, though I hate to say it:
With the record there won't be a player to play it.
No phonograph goes with the phonograph disc,
Which does carry with it an obvious risk.

But the creature to find it would have to be smart,
Would have to have some technological art.
Our scientists say that whoever it is
Will have to rely on the mind that is his.

And finding the record and knowing what's known
Will just have to build a hi-fi of his own.

Perhaps when he does, he will wonder and fear:
"Lord of the Universe, what have we here?
"What kind of spirit has put down so much
And reached out across the vast spaces to touch?"
Or perhaps he will find it and on the same day
Will see it, not hear it, and toss it away.

There's plenty of it to be had,
And some is good and some is bad,
But it is always worth the price.
I speak, of course, of free advice.

Advice and Self-Help

Dr. Osgood's Formula for
Longevity and Loneliness

I'm sure you must have noticed that
The foods you like will make you fat.
And things that you might like to do
Are immoral and illegal, too.

And though we do not have the answer
To what may be the cause of cancer,
A lot of things around the house
When tested on some rat or mouse
Turn out to be bad news, indeed.
So, obviously, what we need
Is a comprehensive list today
Of things from which to stay away.

Hypertension's bad for you, so stay away from stress.
And live an orderly routine, or you will be a mess.
Be sure that you get ample sleep and exercise and such.
But do not overdo it; you must not move or sleep too much.

The "battle of the bulge" it is important that you win.
So don't gain weight, unless of course you're already too thin.
Avoid exciting sports events or literary matter—
Anything that makes your little heart go pitter-patter.

The pace of modern living's made us into nervous wrecks
And one must guard against becoming too obsessed with sex.
Do not read or watch TV, they're both bad for your eyes.
Do not go into a saloon or hang out with the guys.
And before you grab a bottle to pour yourself a drink,
Stop and reconsider, put that bottle down and think.

Although the booze may cause you to be loose and feel no pain,
It is permanently damaging the cells inside your brain.
And in a Chinese restaurant, don't pick from Column B,
Or Column A, for that matter, they're both full of MSG.

And corned beef and salami, though they taste great when you
    bite,
Contain such awful stuff as sodium nitrate and nitrite.
In fact, with all the chemicals, though it may seem incredible,
Almost all the food you eat is totally inedible.

There's fluoride in the reservoirs so that your teeth won't rot.
But that, I have been told by some, is a Communistic plot.
There's cholesterol in beef and eggs, and lots of it in milk,
So keep away from dairy foods and goodies of that ilk.

Steer clear of all cholesterol and foodstuffs that are fried.
People who have eaten them eventually died.
Eschew all forms of violence and turn the other cheek.
But make sure you don't get pushed around. It's no good to be
    weak.
And save your money carefully, but don't be mean or cheap,
For he who hesitates is lost, but look before you leap.

Stay out of cars, for they are quite unsafe at any speed,
And out of planes—to mention them I'm sure I do not need.
But if you walk to somewhere, then I wish you lots of luck.
For walking is a good way to get run down by a truck.

So do not travel anywhere. Suppress the urge to roam.
But remember that most accidents occur right in the home.
Do not go to concerts. If you plan to, call it off.
Did you ever hear a concert where the people didn't cough?
And coughing is unhealthy, for it tends to spread the germs.
With this your doctor will agree in no uncertain terms.

Anywhere there is a crowd that some attraction pleases
You'll hear not only coughs, but also snorts and sneezes.
And while we're on that subject, I have to tell you this:
Another way that germs get spread is when two people kiss.

So do not kiss your girl friend, and never kiss your wife.
And both of you will have a longer, if a duller, life.

And never must you fool around or tell a dirty joke.
And it's all but suicidal a cigarette to smoke.

One must not be a sourpuss while up there on the shelf.
Express yourself, by all means, but keep it to yourself.
Forget the self-indulgences and vices you adore,
For life—if lived correctly—is a long but crashing bore.

But do not bother with a list of things that you must never,
Just stay away from everything—and you will live forever.

It's a Treat to Beat Your Feet on the Mediator's Mud

If A and B have a dispute,
And both are firm and resolute,
If A and B don't get along,
If B thinks A is always wrong,
And A thinks B in many ways
Is out of line and out of phase,
How, then, can one intercede
To fill the role both clearly need?
Of finding them some common ground
Where none is clearly to be found?

It can be done, and what is more,
It's already been done before.
A diplomat—let's call him K—
In years gone by was heard to say,
"To be a mediator great,
One must learn to obfuscate,
To muddy up the water so,
That neither side is apt to know
That what he's just said yes indeed to
Is not at all what's been agreed to.
Nor is it what the other thinks
As into the morass he sinks."

In dealing with some sticky issue
So complicated that you wish you
Could find a way to somehow see
How two opponents might agree
The uninitiated slob
Might see the mediator's job
As making things so clear and grand
That everyone would understand.
Of simplifying, making plain,
Straightforward language to explain,
Exactly what the problem is.

So each side can tell where his
Interest lies, and what will be
Should he happen to agree
To item six, subsection J,
And what each sentence tries to say.

Simplistic theory might suggest
That contracts will work out the best
Whose paragraphs—for ill or good—
Are absolutely understood.
But more sophisticated thought
Has in recent effort taught
That when an issue's really tough,
Clarity is not enough.
It may seem quite an incongruity
What one needs is ambiguity.
And what is least inclined to fail of
Is what one can't make head nor tail of.

Negotiations of all sorts
Find sustenance and life supports
In fuzziness and in confusion,
Obfuscation in profusion.
It only causes hesitation
To understand the situation.

So if a treaty you'd arrive at
The wording one should really strive at
Is that which has a pleasant ring
And doesn't mean a bloody thing.
The great advantage there, you see,
Is helping both sides to agree.
Each side's interpretation is
That its thinking jibes with his.
It only plants the seeds of doubt
To go and spell the meaning out.

If logic seems a bit elusive,
Provisions mutually exclusive.

Muddy water everywhere
It's quite all right, do not despair.
It's not at all your blame or fault
If somehow you can't fathom SALT.
If you feel lost out in the bog,
Your vision hampered by the fog,
So you can't tell what you're opposed to
Be advised—you're not supposed to.
A diplomat, both great and wise,
To reach agreement always tries.
And if the sides refuse to budge,
The proper thing to do is fudge.

Expert Tease

The world is full of experts, but with every breaking story,
The experts seem a whole lot like Professor Irwin Corey.
Because they are authorities, they stand out from the throng,
The problem being that they are so very often wrong.

Authorities and experts have a certain predilection
To certify their expertise with forecasts and predictions.
Analysts of every sort, from Wall Street to psychologists,
Political observers, and TV meteorologists,
Are consulted as were once the ancient prophets, seers, and
    soothsayers,
Even though we know darn well they're not exactly truth sayers.
Not because they wish to tell us things that are not so;
It's only that, like you and me, they really do not know.

Economic experts read the entrails of statistics,
Predicting what will happen next, as if they were all mystics.
And if it doesn't work out just the way that they foresaw,
They say, "Well, it sure ought to be. There ought to be a law!"
The best of the prognosticators learn a little trick
By which, when they prognosticate, they somehow seem to pick
Events that are inevitable, made somehow to sound
As if in the prediction there is something quite profound.

Surely, then, as followeth the night upon the day,
The market will reverse itself and turn the other way.
And though it is quite difficult to pinpoint for you when,
It will do so when it's ready. Not a moment before then.
Consultants gather fancy fees for such advice as this;
And, hedging in the things they say, they hardly ever miss.
And so it is, you'll hear the thought that, on Election Day,
We will have an election, and the voters have their say.
And observers of the world are given now and then to mention
That war will come to pass unless there's lessening of tension.

The future lies before us, and the younger generation
Will inherit what we do; they are the future of the nation.

The rain will stop, and when it does, the skies will then be sunny,
And the government is spending altogether too much money.
Wise men know that fate is a phenomenon of whim,
And reading what it says is going way out on a limb.
So, what you have to learn to do, and learn rather fast,
Is to fearlessly predict events that happened in the past.

That is to say, you nod and smile when happenings unfold,
And you say you knew it all along, but it could not be told
Because of this and that and something else you can't reveal.
But now the truth is out, they dealt the hand you knew they'd
    deal.
How many times have you been told by someone that he knew
That Nixon would resign because he knew that he was through?
And that he would get a pardon from someone, sometime,
    somehow.
It was all inevitable, that's what they say now.

When Wall Street tumbles, experts always have a reason why.
It happened because Jimmy Carter stubbed his toe, they sigh.
And should it have gone up, you see, that very selfsame day,
Why, they knew the stub was coming and discounted it, they'd say.
Ex post facto forecasting is what you have to do
If you want to be an expert and have folks consulting you.

And now, here is my forecast for the week that is to come.
The news that will be breaking will be quite a shock to some.
The president will meet at times with several of his aides,
And one thing will develop as the other issue fades.
And seven days will come and go as these events occur,
And you and I will be a whole week older than we were.
And if we do not have a drink, we'll likely raise a thirst.
Just remember, when it comes to pass, it was here you heard it first.

Better Than Ever, But Worse Than Before

One of the nice things about the world is that everything keeps improving all the time. Have you noticed that? The urge never to let well enough alone has brought us ever-newer and ever-more-improved products and services, the latest of which is that the Postal Service now wants to improve the Zoning Improvement Plan (otherwise known as the ZIP system) by adding four more digits to the present five-digit codes so the Postal Service can be even more wonderful and improved than it is already. And you and I will have the chance to improve our memories by remembering nine ZIP digits instead of five—076434291, let us say.

A hundred and twenty-five years ago, when Otis invented the elevator, an improvement was really an improvement. The elevator was a good idea, although the doctors now tell us that walking up and down the stairs used to be good for people. But at some point they improved the elevator by replacing the elevator operator with buttons so that you can run the elevator yourself. A lot of improvements are that way. The phone company thinks it is a great improvement that you now have to place your own long-distance calls, instead of having an operator do it. A major airline is now promoting a terrific improvement in baggage handling, which is that you carry your bags on and off the plane yourself.

Just when you think that they've about run out of improvements, along comes another one. As you know, Amtrak, which was created to improve railroad passenger service, has improved passenger railroad service so much that there hardly is any passenger railroad service anymore. Every time Amtrak comes along with what it calls an improvement, it means cutting out more service and reducing the number of passenger trains and cities served. And the Postal Service, which has done all that it has done so far in the name of improvement, now routes mail all over creation to get it from Point A to Point B, makes fewer deliveries a day, proposes *fewer* delivery days in the week, and it often takes a letter longer to get from here to there than it used to—but at greatly increased cost, of course. My, it's just an inspiration the way those folks have improved things!

Food is greatly improved now, as you well know. Tomatoes, for example, have been improved so much that they now have no taste at all, and a texture like cardboard. Clothes have been so improved, what with double-knit polyesters and all, that a whole new family of products has emerged to deal with static cling.

Why, almost every area you can think of has been improved. With the benefit of electronics and audiovisual aids, with sophisticated professional teaching techniques, we have so improved the educational system in this country that some of our college students don't even need to take the improved remedial reading courses that universities now offer. The improved, hand-held calculators mean kids don't need to add and subtract anymore. Good thing, too, since they can't.

Government has really improved, as the candidates running for office down through the years have assured us it would. It's just hard to imagine how everybody got along without the agencies and bureaus that we now have to improve things. Congress is in there improving away, session after session. Expensive? Sure, but look at how improved it all is. Streamlined, too. And efficient. That's why we have the GSA to streamline and improve the way government agencies do things and, of course, to make sure everything is on the up and up. Taxes, especially, are up and up.

Sometimes you get obstructionists who want to stand in the way of improvement and progress, of course. There'll always be somebody who doesn't want to have to use two hands to read his digital watch . . . who doesn't find easy-opening cans that easy to open . . . who prefers country roads to superhighways . . . who can't stand all the convenience provided by convenient household appliances. There are even some people who don't prefer the way television has improved and would rather sit and talk or read a book. But there's no stopping progress. Excelsior! Onward and upward, ad infinitum. Or is it ad nauseam?

In Words of One Syllable

The following is a commencement address given by the author at Saint Bonaventure University in 1976.

If I were you, if I were you,
Let me tell you what I'd do.
I'd show the world a thing or two,
If I were you, if I were you.

I'd work so hard, I would not tire,
I'm sure I'd set the world on fire.
So go and do what I would do,
If I were you, if I were you.

At all times I'd be fair and just,
And yet I'd do the things I must
To get to where I mean to go,
Which is to say On Top, you know.

If I were you, I do not think
That I would curse or smoke or drink.
I'd shun all forms of sin and vice.
I'd be so fine and good and nice.

I'd be on time, I'd not be late,
The sort of guy you love to hate.
The world that waits just past those gates
Is made for clean and brand new slates.

I mean to say, it's meant for you.
And it is right that you should do
Great deeds, for here you have been taught
What great men did, what great minds thought.

I'm sure that I would do them, too,
If I were you, if I were you.
As luck would have it, I am not.
I'm stuck with me and what I've got.

No brand new slate for such as I,
And since that's so, I can't see why
There's any need for me to do
Those things I would if I were you.

I'll just go on the way I was,
With faults and all, the way one does.
The sense of this, I'm sure you'd see
If you were me, if you were me.

Go do the good things that I say
And I will cheer you all the way.
But, ah, to think what I would do,
If I were you, if I were you.

Charles Osgood was born in New York City in 1933. He grew up in Baltimore, Philadelphia, and New Jersey. At college (Fordham), he majored not in journalism but in economics. This left him with certain ideas about economics, some of which are in this book. Osgood spent his military career in the U.S. Army Band, and his professional years at WGMS in Washington; WHCT in Hartford, Connecticut; ABC, and now CBS, where he divides his time as a news correspondent between radio and television.